"Hi there, it was a masculine voice

Láni opened her eyes and gasped—a hairy shin was directly in her line of vision. She sank lower in the *furo*. "What are you doing here?"

"I was planning to have a soak before dinner," Wes said, crouching by the tub. "Unless it would make you uncomfortable."

"No, of course not," she lied, casually shrugging her shoulders. She could see his right thigh where his cotton robe fell away. If she looked any higher...

Wes grinned, openly staring at Lani's sinuous shape in the dark water.

"Well!" she snapped. "Stop staring at me as if you were at some peep show! Get in or get out!"

Peep show! He'd give her a peep show, all right. He stood. "I have to shower first," he said, flinging off his robe. Lani clamped her eyes shut ... then opened them a crack.

She earned herself a peek at his broad bare back, his long, hard-muscled legs and his untanned rear end as he stepped into the shower and banged the door closed behind him.

Candace Schuler, popular Temptation author, has already written six Temptations and plans another two for 1989. An avid traveler, she has collected not only mementos, but also research notes from her visits to the most exotic places. *Almost Paradise* is set in heavenly Hawaii, where Candace and her husband lived for a short while—before they set out to sail the high seas for several months. As a result of that experience, sailing is something she knows well— almost as well as she knows how to tell a sensuous story about two people sharing the same dreams.

Books by Candace Schuler

HARLEQUIN TEMPTATION

Don't miss any of our special offers. Write to us at the following address for information on our newest releases.

Harlequin Reader Service
901 Fuhrmann Blvd., P.O. Box 1397, Buffalo, NY 14240
Canadian address: P.O. Box 603,
Fort Erie, Ont. L2A 5X3

Almost Paradise

CANDACE SCHULER

Harlequin Books

TORONTO • NEW YORK • LONDON
AMSTERDAM • PARIS • SYDNEY • HAMBURG
STOCKHOLM • ATHENS • TOKYO • MILAN

To my father,
Denzil Darwin Schnabel, U.S.N., Retired,
because it's his favorite

and to my grandmother,
Evalena Kittle Schnabel MacBeth,
who was as indomitable in her own way
as the fictional Sumiko

Published May 1989

ISBN 0-373-25350-8

1

LANI MACPHERSON PUT THE PHONE down with exaggerated care, an expression of annoyance on her tanned face. "Great," she said aloud, her fingers still resting on the yellow receiver. "This is just great!"

Barely two o'clock in the afternoon and her grandmother expected her to drop everything—just close up the office and leave!—to rush to the rescue of Gerard Adams. The seemingly omnipotent, all powerful Gerard Adams, the family lawyer who Gran was expecting to . . . to *something*, Lani thought, shaking her head with half-amused exasperation. She drew her hand away from the phone and reached under the desk for her canvas tote bag. She didn't know what Gran expected him to do, exactly, but she did know that she wasn't going to like it.

And she sure as hell didn't have time for it.

There was a bank statement among the pile of papers in her In basket that desperately needed to be reconciled to the company checkbook, a ledger in the middle right drawer of the desk that hadn't been balanced for over a month, and an invoice for two hundred feet of anchor chain, when she'd only ordered a hundred, that needed to be argued about with her supplier. Not to mention the yellow phone on her desk that would surely ring more than once this afternoon. And now, just as there had been too many times in the five months since her father's death, there would only be the recorded message on a machine to answer it.

Rich, her only full-time employee, wouldn't be back from the two-week charter until sometime tomorrow and Kim, her new part-time office helper, didn't come in until after three o'clock when the local high school let out. But did her grandmother consider any of that?

No, of course not! She just called, making her request in that quiet how-can-you-possibly-refuse-me voice of hers, and Lani found herself locking up the small two-room office facing Ala Wai Harbor and hopping into her battered yellow Jeep like a trained seal, off on her dutiful way to rescue Gerard Adams from the vagaries of her grandmother's ancient Mercedes sedan.

And it was all for no reason, she fumed silently as she tucked her hair up under the red baseball cap that kept it out of her eyes when she drove. She slipped a pair of oversized yellow-framed sunglasses on her nose and leaned forward, turning the key in the ignition with more force than was strictly necessary.

Gran's bringing the family lawyer out from San Francisco wasn't going to change a thing. Not a thing! Sail Away Tours was hers and there was nothing anyone—not Gran, not Gerard Adams, not the mighty power of the law itself—could do. It was *hers*, lock, stock and life preservers, left to her by the completely legitimate dictates of her father's will. What her grandmother thought Gerard Adams could do about it was beyond Lani's comprehension. But, then, she thought, merging into the stream of traffic that clogged Ala Moana Boulevard, lots of things her grandmother did were beyond her comprehension.

For despite having married a Westerner, and despite having lived the last forty-five years of her life in the Western world, Sumiko Walsh was still essentially a traditional, Old World Japanese gentlewoman. And she believed in being as inscrutable as that ancient and honorable race had long been reputed to be. She also believed that Lani shouldn't be running Sail Away Tours, at least not so directly, so that she was involved in the day-to-day operations. It was unlady-like and unnecessary and, mostly, it kept her from getting married and producing the great-grandchildren that Su-miko thought were her due.

"Don't hold your breath, Gran," Lani muttered to her-self, brushing irritably at the blowing strands of dark glossy hair that had escaped her baseball cap. She scowled at the slow-moving car ahead of her, her brow furrowed as she mentally argued with her grandmother.

Slavish devotion to a man, no matter how well loved, just wasn't in the cards for her. It never had been. When she got married, it would be to a man who shared her love of the sea and who would be, if not a partner in her charter sail-ing business, at least understanding and supportive of it. The man in her life, whoever he eventually turned out to be, would be her partner, *not* her lord and master.

And not any time soon, in any case. She was only twenty-five; there was plenty of time for love and marriage and all that went with it. Right now she didn't need the distrac-tion, or the complications that a man would add to her life. She had all the complications she could handle just run-ning her business.

"If I still have a business after today," she grumbled aloud, glancing at the waterproof tank watch on her wrist. Ten minutes had already gone by, and she had barely moved more than a few blocks down the busy Honolulu boule-vard.

Damn! Why couldn't Gran's chauffeur just have called a taxi on the car phone when the Mercedes broke down? And why in hell wasn't the traffic moving?

There was no answer to her first question but the sight of a bronzed teenager, his sun-bleached hair blowing behind him as he maneuvered around the car ahead of her on a skateboard, answered her second. Dozens of gorgeous flower leis hung around his neck and dangled from his arms. He was selling them car-to-car, holding up traffic as the drivers made their purchases.

Irritably Lani tooted her horn at him.

The boy looked up, smiled, and with a slight push of one foot, propelled himself toward her. "Well, hey, you delicious little wahine, you," he hollered, using the Hawaiian word for girl. White teeth gleamed at her as he came to a stop beside her car. "Wanna lei?" He wriggled his eyebrows suggestively.

Lani ignored the double entendre. "No thanks." She nosed the Jeep forward a bit, keeping up with the creeping line of traffic. The boy and the skateboard rolled along beside her. "I'm in kind of a hurry," she said. "Got to go pick up—"

"Goin' to the airport, huh?" he interrupted, jumping to the obvious conclusion. "Then you do need a lei. I thought so. Here." He lowered his arm, shook a fragrant lei into his hand, then held it up. "One of my prettiest ones," he said, turning it for her inspection. "Fifteen dollars."

"Fifteen dollars?" Lani's eyes opened wide. "That's highway robbery!"

"For you," he reconsidered, "I'll make it twelve."

Lani shook her head. "I'm not going to the—"

"Ten," he said, reaching out to put one hand on the side of the Jeep. "That's as low as I can go and still make a profit."

"I'm sorry, I—"

"All right, nine. But that's my absolute, final offer."

Lani shook her head again, but her "No" was drowned out by the car horn that blared behind them.

"Aw, keep your pants on," the boy hollered, not even looking around. "Eight," he said to Lani.

The horn sounded behind them again, louder this time, and longer. Lani frowned into her rearview mirror. The driver lifted his hand to honk again.

"You're holdin' up traffic here." He jiggled the lei at her. "Eight dollars," he said.

The one blaring horn became two. The boy's hand was still on the side of her Jeep.

"Okay, okay. I'll take it." She reached into the tote bag on the seat beside her. "Here." She pressed a ten dollar bill into his hand. He dropped the lei over the side of the Jeep onto her lap. "Keep the change," she said, but he had already let go of the Jeep to zero in on his next hapless victim.

"You bandit," she muttered under her breath, but she smiled, the fingers of one tanned hand drifting down to touch the delicate flowers in her lap before she reached for the gearshift.

One certainly had to admire the kid's business sense, she thought, ignoring the grinding complaint of the transmission as she shifted into first, even if his tactics did resemble those of a hungry barracuda circling a school of fish. A sharp operator like him probably wouldn't have the trouble she'd been having with Sail Away's books. He'd probably been born knowing how to handle money. Whereas she . . .

Well, she shrugged, it was too late to worry about that now. She'd learn. Just like she was learning about keeping the bookings straight and ordering supplies and hiring competent staff. Slowly, maybe, and with a mistake or two—or twenty, she thought, smiling wryly—but she'd learn.

"Because Sail Away is mine," she said to herself as if the words were a talisman. "And I'm going to keep it and run it. Just like Pop wanted me to. Just like I've always planned."

And she would tell Gerard Adams that, too, in no uncertain terms the minute she saw him. Maybe he'd see that his harebrained mission—whatever it was—was hopeless. Maybe he'd let her take him back to the airport instead of to her grandmother's house. Maybe. But she doubted it. When Sumiko Walsh sent out an SOS, Gerard Adams usually came running. Figuratively anyway. Much as she might wish it, this time was probably no different.

Lani sighed and straightened behind the wheel of the Jeep, her black eyes scanning the road for her grandmother's classic navy blue Mercedes. She saw it a few miles farther on, pulled over off the road with a tow truck already parked in front of it. Three men in earnest discussion were standing between the two vehicles. Lani passed the stranded car, made an illegal U-turn and came back. She pulled up behind the Mercedes and tapped her horn lightly. The three men looked up. One of them was her grandmother's elderly chauffeur, Hiroshi. The second one was obviously the tow truck operator. And the third one was a complete stranger.

Lani squinted and leaned forward over the steering wheel, her black eyes narrowing behind the lenses of her sunglasses. Well, whoever he was, she decided, he definitely *wasn't* Gerard Adams.

The Gerard Adams she knew was a tall, distinguished man with a full head of silvery gray hair and a penchant for fine English-tailored business suits. He was also quite elderly. Seventy-one, if she remembered correctly. And, while this man was certainly as tall as her grandmother's lawyer, he was definitely younger. Much younger, she thought, her eyes skimming over his broad shoulders and firm, lean torso. He wasn't silver-haired, either. Nor was he wearing an English-tailored business suit. But he was coming toward her, she realized. His long legs covered the short distance between them, rounding the rear bumper of the disabled Mercedes with the confident, unconscious swagger of a buccaneer on the rolling deck of a ship.

Lani pulled off her baseball cap, tossing it on the seat beside her tote bag, and swung her long, bare legs over the side of the Jeep to meet him—whoever he was—with her feet planted firmly on the ground. The forgotten lei slithered downward at her abrupt movement. She grabbed it, started to toss it on the seat, then, remembering its delicate fragility, draped it around her neck instead. It brushed her sunglasses as she lowered it over her head, knocking them askew, and she took those off, too, negligently dropping them onto the seat beside her cap as she turned to greet the tall, broad-shouldered man who had come to a stop less than two feet in front of her. She had to tilt her head back to see his face.

"Miss MacPherson?"

"Ms," she corrected automatically, and looked up into the most intensely blue eyes she had ever seen. They smiled at her.

"Ms MacPherson, then," he said.

Lani quite frankly stared. He was, bar none, the best looking man she'd ever laid eyes on. On the far side of thirty, she decided, judging by the tiny lines radiating from the corners of his remarkably blue eyes. He was at least a head taller than her own five foot four, his broad shoulders covered by the pale blue material of an open-throated knit pullover. His hair was light brown and sun-streaked, as if he spent much of his time outdoors. It curled riotously around his head, making a soft frame for a hard, square chin, a strong, straight nose, and a shapely, faintly sensual mouth. A small, thin scar curled over and under his right jaw, startlingly white against his tanned skin.

Lani thought of pirates—sea chests full of pieces of eight and plundered gems—tall sailing ships flying the Jolly Roger—captive maidens cowering in a delicious state of excitement and fear under the sparkling blue gaze of a sun-bronzed captain.

The object of her appraisal returned her stare as silently as she gave it. His Uncle Gerard had said she was small, he thought, looking down at her with the smile still in his eyes. And she was. Just a little bit of a thing, really; the top of her head barely reached his shoulder. But she most definitely wasn't "just a little girl."

Her glossy hair was the deep, rich, red-black color of overripe cherries and was cut in a sophisticated chin-length bob that took full advantage of its shine and texture. Her eyes were huge and black with an intriguingly exotic, faintly mysterious tilt to them. And there were grown-up curves hidden under the flowery drawstring shorts and the fragrant lei around her neck.

The smile in his blue eyes deepened, reaching down to curve his lips. Oh, she was little, all right, he thought, as dainty as a porcelain doll, but every inch a woman.

"Well?" he said then, feeling it was time to break their silent stare. If it went on much longer it would be embarrassing.

Lani's brows pulled together in a frown. "You're not Gerard Adams," she blurted.

"No, I'm not." A sun-kissed eyebrow lifted slightly at the tone of accusation in her voice. "I'm Wes Adams. Gerard is my uncle."

"Uncle?"

"Uncle." He answered her as if she had really asked a question. "As in the brother of one's parent . . ."

But Lani wasn't listening.

Gerard's nephew, she was thinking, her mind suddenly going a mile a minute. Gerard's tall, good-looking nephew. She wondered if he was a lawyer, too. And if he were single. "Gran was expecting your uncle," she said. *Or was she?* "He was going to take care of a business matter for her."

"And I'm going to take care of it now," he informed her. "It was decided that the junior partner of Adams & Adams could handle this particular problem."

Lani sighed loudly. So he *was* a lawyer. She'd give ten to one he was single, too. She glanced down at his left hand. No ring. A terrible suspicion began forming in her mind. *Please, don't let me be right*, she prayed silently. *I don't need the aggravation.*

"Gran's not going to be pleased," she said, already fearing in her heart that it wasn't true. Sumiko Walsh was probably bubbling over with pleasure right this very minute. "She was expecting the senior partner."

"No, she wasn't," Wes said. "She was expecting me."

With that, Lani's suspicions solidified into an absolute certainty. "To do what?" she asked, her eyes speculative and suspicious.

Wes shrugged. "She has some inventory problems at Walsh Imports."

"Is that all?" Disbelief and sarcasm warred in her tone.

"All I'm going to tell you." A teasing gleam lit his blue eyes as he looked down at her. "As you grandmother's legal counsel, I'm not at liberty to say more than that."

Lani snorted inelegantly. "You don't really believe there's an inventory problem at Walsh Imports that requires your expert legal attention, do you?" The look she gave him suggested that, surely, he couldn't be that stupid.

"Yes, I really do," Wes answered easily. "That's why I'm here." And it was, mostly. The leave of absence he intended taking after he'd handled Sumiko Walsh's problem wasn't anyone's business but his own.

But Lani was already shaking her head. "No, you're not."

"I'm not?"

"No. You're here because—" She hesitated, assailed by sudden doubt.

"Yes?" he prompted. "Because?"

She hesitated. What if she was wrong?

But, no, she thought. She knew her grandmother *was* matchmaking. It was as plain as the nose on her face. But with him standing there, looking down at her with that inquiring, lawyerlike expression on his handsome face, she suddenly felt foolish putting it into words. Because maybe, just maybe, she was wrong. And then she'd feel like a complete idiot.

"Because why?" he prompted again, intrigued by the glimmer of embarrassment in her dark eyes.

Lani shook her head again and looked away, over to where Hiroshi and the tow truck operator were haggling about how to best hoist the Mercedes. "Nothing."

"Now wait just a minute," Wes protested. "You can't make a statement like that and then just say 'nothing.' Why do you think I'm in Hawaii?"

"I'm sure my grandmother will tell you," she said, still not looking at him. She was sure her grandmother wouldn't, but she no longer cared to amend the oversight. Let him find out on his own.

"Not good enough. I want you to tell me." There was a note of command in his voice.

Lani's eyes flashed back to his, her eyebrows lifted haughtily. But Wes wasn't intimidated in the least. His implacable blue eyes looked back at her, waiting for an answer to his question.

But what answer could she give him that wouldn't sound like something out of a bad Victorian novel?

"Well?" he demanded.

Lani took a deep breath. It was obvious that he wasn't going to take no for an answer. "My grandmother thinks I need a diversion," she said, willing herself not to blush.

"A diversion? Would you care to elaborate on that?" There was barely concealed amusement in his voice, and in his eyes, too, but he managed not to snicker.

Lani's own eyes narrowed. "I think my meaning is fairly obvious."

Wes said nothing, deliberately creating a silence for her to fill.

"My grandmother is playing matchmaker between you and me," Lani said, filling it. "Is that elaborate enough for you?"

"Why?"

"Why what?"

"Why do you think your grandmother is playing matchmaker?"

"I don't *think* she's playing matchmaker," she snapped. "I know it. And you'll know it, too, as soon as you've talked to Dave Yamazaki." Dave was the man who ran Walsh Imports for Sumiko. "My grandmother hasn't got a problem at Walsh Imports, inventory or otherwise, that needs your attention."

"She doesn't?"

"No, she doesn't. Her only problem is me, Mr. Adams. And Sail Away Tours."

"Sail Away Tours?"

"My charter sailing business," she informed him. *As if you didn't know.*

"You have a charter sailing business?" He knew there was some sort of sailing business in the family but he'd never envisioned it being run by a little bit of a thing like her. Her father ran it, didn't he? Then he remembered her father was dead.

"Yes, *I* have a charter sailing business," Lani mimicked, exasperated. She flapped a hand at the front of the yellow T-shirt she wore. Her fingers brushed against the lei. Without thinking, she lifted it over her head so he could see the lettering on her T-shirt. "See?"

Wes saw. The words, Sail Away Tours, curved in a half circle above her breasts. Experiences For The Adventurous formed the bottom half of the circle below them. The stylized outline of a schooner filled the center, the top of the rear mast coming precisely to the point of her right nipple. She was obviously braless under the T-shirt; the soft yellow cotton faithfully delineated the small, pert shape of her.

Wes swallowed. *Definitely all woman.* "Your sailing business?" he said inanely, his eyes glued to the front of her T-shirt. "What's your sailing business got to do with Walsh Imports?"

"Ab—" Lani licked suddenly dry lips. "Absolutely nothing," she managed, resisting the urge to cover her breasts with her hands. So she was braless, she told herself. So what? Unless she had a bathing suit on, she was usually braless; she had very little to put in a bra.

So why was he staring at her like that?

"Sail Away Tours is *my* business," she said, but her voice was less firm than she would have liked. "And there's nothing anyone can do to take it away from me."

"Who said anyone's trying?" he countered. He looked away from her chest to where the front end of the Mercedes was finally being hoisted into the air, then back again, his eyes drawn as if against his will.

"I say someone's trying," she said shakily, watching him watching her. "But Sail Away's mine," she said again, trying to ignore the fluttery feeling in her stomach, the sudden racing of her blood. "And it will stay mine. I'm not about to be discouraged or diverted from running it. So you might as well turn around and go home."

Wes said nothing; he was wondering how her breasts would feel if he reached out and touched them.

"Did you hear me?" Lani demanded then, embarrassed and annoyed and excited all at once. She didn't have time for this! None of it! Not the embarrassment or the annoyance and especially not the delicious, traitorous excitement that was bubbling through her blood. "I said I won't be diverted."

"That's all very—" Wes blinked and tried again, managing, at last, to look away from her chest. He focused on her flushed face instead. "That's all very, ah, interesting," he said, thinking that the view wasn't any less stimulating. "But what does it have to do with me?"

"It has everything to do with you." Lani lifted her hands to emphasize the point. The lei swayed with her movement, trailing the sweet scent of ginger flowers in its wake. "Everything! Because my grandmother has you in mind as the diversion, Mr. Adams!"

"I'm the diversion, huh?" He was silent a moment, pondering all the ramifications of that. He'd never been considered a diversion before. And then he smiled. It was a teasing smile. A knowing smile. A decadent, all-male, Machiavellian smile.

"Well, in that case—" Wes reached out and captured her chin between thumb and finger. Her skin was silky smooth and warm. "Since it looks like we're destined to be friends," he drawled, with a slight emphasis on the last word. "Shouldn't you call me Wes?"

Lani jerked her chin out of his grasp. "We are *not* going to be friends."

"No?"

"No!"

"Sure?"

"Positive," she said firmly, trying to ignore the insidious heat generated by his touch. She took a careful step back, out of his reach. "We aren't going to be friends. Not now. Not ever."

"Maybe not now," he conceded generously. "But you'll change your mind when you get to know me better." His voice was confiding and somehow suggestive. "I'm a real likable guy when you get to know me."

Lani took another half step back, away from the intimacy in his tone, and felt the Jeep come up against her rear. She straightened away from it, refusing to be intimidated. "I don't care how likable you are," she said, her chin lifting to an imperious angle. "I haven't got the slightest interest in getting to know you better." It was a lie.

"Never?" He managed with that one word, despite his size and overpowering maleness and the wicked smile that lingered along the edges of his mouth, to sound like a small boy denied what he wanted most.

Lani tried to resist that look. She tried hard, instinctively knowing that he was using it deliberately to charm and cajole, but a small answering smile tugged at her lips. "Oh, don't be ridiculous," she said, suddenly seeing the absurdity of the whole situation. After all, he wasn't responsible for her grandmother's idiotic matchmaking schemes; he was just as much an innocent victim as she was.

Wasn't he?

"Look," she said earnestly. "I just meant that we aren't going to be friends the way my grandmother thinks we're going to be friends. We'll just be . . . friends." Her shoulders lifted in a little shrug. "Okay?"

"Okay," Wes agreed, wondering if he really did. Simple friendship was a far cry from what he was feeling at the moment. Rampant lust was more like it.

They stood there, staring at each other for a long, silent, strangely intimate second, sparks of attraction and interest bouncing between them like a Ping-Pong ball gone wild until the chauffeur's voice broke the spell.

"We are ready to go, Missy Lani," he called as he came around the rear of the Mercedes. Its nose was in the air now, the front bumper securely fastened to the tow truck's boom line.

Lani dragged her eyes away from Wes's. "Ready?" she said to the chauffeur.

The Oriental man bowed slightly. "All ready," he affirmed, popping open the trunk of the Mercedes. "I get Mr. Adams-san's luggage now," he said, tagging the Japanese honorific onto Wes's last name. "Put it in your Jeep, okay?"

"Yes, of course. Thank you, Hiroshi."

"Very good, Missy Lani," he said, scurrying past her toward the rear of the open Jeep, a briefcase in one hand, a Pullman suitcase in the other, the strap of a folding garment bag slung over one shoulder. He lifted them into the back of the Jeep, setting them on top of a battered metal tackle box and a pile of damp orange life preservers. "Please to tell Mrs. Walsh-san that I will make haste to return," he said.

"Yes, I will. Thank you, Hiroshi."

He bowed again, then hurried around to the passenger side of the tow truck. The door creaked open with a squeal of protesting hinges, then slammed shut. The engine roared to life. The driver accelerated into the traffic.

"Well," said Lani, looking anywhere but at Wes. "I guess we'd better get going, too."

"Mm-hm," he agreed, but he didn't move. Instead his eyes wandered over her still flushed face, down to where her breasts pressed against the soft cotton of her T-shirt, to the lei still dangling from her hand. "Is that for me?"

"What?" Lani followed the direction of his gaze. "Oh, this. Yes. Yes, it is." She held the flower necklace up in both hands so that it fell into an open circle between them. "Bend down a little," she instructed, raising herself on tiptoe. In the timeless Hawaiian gesture of welcome, she lifted it over his bent head. "Aloha, Wes Adams," she said. "Welcome to Hawaii."

He felt the soft skin of her inner arms brush against his ears as she dropped the flowers into place. He caught the faint scents of sandalwood and roses beneath the stronger one of the flowers. A small, very male smile turned up the corners of his mouth. A not-quite-teasing spark lit up his blue eyes. "Isn't it traditional to get a kiss with one of these?" he said blandly.

For a scant second, a heartbeat only, Lani considered lifting her mouth to the temptation of his. And then she thought better of it. "Don't press your luck, friend!" she said, scowling at him instead.

2

THEY COVERED THE FIRST fifteen minutes of the drive with no further conversation except brief exchanges about the length of Wes's flight, the present weather conditions in both Hawaii and San Francisco and the possible reason for the breakdown of the Mercedes, then, having thoroughly exhausted the topics, fell silent for the next ten minutes.

Lani had expected him to say something about her grandmother's matchmaking scheme. Or to ask about her business. Or make some comment about the way the gears ground when she shifted into first. But he didn't.

He was slouched in his seat, his knees against the dashboard, his head thrown back, looking for all the world as if he intended to nap.

Which is just fine with me, Lani told herself. Her orders, after all, were to deliver him to her grandmother. And the less conversation they had on the way there, the better—despite whatever it was that had happened between them back there on the side of the road. *Or because of whatever had happened,* she added truthfully, darting a glance at him out of the corner of her eye.

Isn't it traditional to get a kiss with one of these? he'd said, and for one dangerous moment she'd found herself actually wanting to kiss him. And wouldn't that have just made her grandmother as happy as a clam!

Oh, well, she thought, reassuring herself—ten minutes more and she'd have him out of her hair. She shifted smoothly into second and turned the Jeep onto the curving road that led to her grandmother's.

It was a gorgeous day, as almost all days were in Hawaii. The balmy air smelled of the sea and a hundred kinds of flowers. The tropical sun slanted under the fringed top of the Jeep, warming her bare arms and legs where it touched them. The sweet, sultry wind whipped around her in the open vehicle, tugging at the tendrils of reddish black hair that escaped her cap, ruffling the petals of the ginger flower lei around her passenger's neck.

"Tell me about Sail Away," Wes said without opening his eyes.

Lani slanted him a quick glance. "What about it?"

"Anything."

"Why?" she said suspiciously.

"Because you've, ah, piqued my interest, let's say." He rolled his head sideways against the seat and opened his eyes. "I'm interested in sailing in general, and I'm curious as to why your grandmother doesn't want you to run this business," he said, staring at her profile. Her small, straight nose all but disappeared beneath her oversized sunglasses; her mouth had the tender curve of an innocent child; her rounded chin was temptingly bite-sized. "After all, she runs Walsh Imports."

Lani shook her head. "Gran *owns* Walsh Imports," she said, downshifting into a curve. "Dave Yamazaki runs it."

"I see. And does she have someone in mind to run Sail Away for you?"

"Rich Billings." The Jeep protested as she changed gears again. Lani ignored it; the Jeep always protested that particular gear change. "He started as a deck hand, oh, about ten years ago, I guess," she went on, her voice pitched to be heard over the rush of wind through the open car. "He was

Pop's favorite first mate after me. And he captains most of the longer charters now."

"And does this Rich Billings want to run Sail Away?"

"Not a chance," she said. "It would cut into his time with the wahines." A wry grin curved her mouth as she spoke, making it suddenly not quite as innocent and childish-looking as it had been just a minute before.

Thank God, Wes thought, and wondered what her lips would taste like under his. He promised himself that he'd make it a point to find out. "A lady's man, huh?"

Lani's grin got wider. "I don't think he wastes his time with ladies."

"And what does your grandmother say to that?"

"She says that the responsibility of running Sail Away would do him good," Lani answered without even stopping to consider the amount of information he was getting out of her with his easy questions. "But that if he doesn't want to, then Al Duffy certainly would." She paused, reaching up with one hand to brush away the strands of hair that blew across her lips. "She's probably right about that," she said. "Al runs the fishing excursions out of Haliewa on the north side of the island. He's been with Sail Away for a long time and he's good at what he does. There was even some talk once about Al buying into Sail Away but . . ." She shrugged.

"But?"

"I don't know what happened, really. Pop never said anything. But I'm glad it never came about."

"Why's that?"

"Al's one of those old salts who believes that a woman doesn't even belong on a boat, let alone running a charter sailing business. I'd find that attitude difficult to cope with if he were a partner."

"It sounds as if you've given it some thought."

"Of course I've given it some thought." She spared him an annoyed glance out of the corner of her eye. "Enough thought to know that I don't want anyone running Sail Away but me. Enough thought so that—" She broke off suddenly, her black eyes narrowing behind the sunglasses. "Why are you asking so many questions?"

Wes's shoulders lifted against the seat. "Just making polite conversation."

"Uh-huh," she said inelegantly. "I'll bet."

"Idle curiosity?" he offered, his eyes crinkling up at the corners.

Lani shook her head.

"Occupational hazard," he admitted, grinning. He'd been wondering how long it would take her to realize she was being pumped for information. "Lawyers are trained to ask questions, you know."

"Well, ask them somewhere else."

"Why should I ask my questions somewhere else?"

"Because I'm not going to answer any more, that's why."

"But I don't—"

"We're here," she said, cutting off his next protest as she turned into the wide gravel drive of the Walsh residence.

The driveway was a half circle bordered on both sides by manicured lawns and waving palm trees. Lush, carefully tended flowerbeds flanked the wide brick walk that led up to the house. Two stone lions guarded the front door, standing sentinel on either side of the elderly Japanese woman who stood at the open threshold, waiting to greet them.

"You're certainly getting the full treatment," Lani remarked to Wes as she climbed out of the Jeep. "One of her best kimonos, no less."

Sumiko Walsh was wearing a black silk kimono with wide sleeve panels reaching nearly to the floor. It was edged all around in pearl gray silk and sashed with a wide gray brocade obi. Her lustrous black hair, only faintly threaded with gray, was more intricately coiled than usual, and she had gone so far as to add two tinkling silver ornaments that danced and sparkled each time she moved her head.

She was giving Wes honored-guest status, Lani realized. Very honored-guest status. The kind of honored-guest status that was usually reserved for a husband's employers or visiting dignitaries, or prospective bridegrooms. *Dream on, Gran,* Lani telegraphed silently, shaking her head at her grandmother's obvious ploy.

"My dear Wesley," Sumiko said softly, bowing from the waist as they came up the steps. "How lovely to see you again."

"It's lovely to see you again, too, Mrs. Walsh-san," he replied, taking her hands in his as he returned her bow. "And how lovely you look." He spread their clasped hands wide, surveying her. "Is all this for me?"

"But of course." She nodded serenely. "I can see that my granddaughter has welcomed you in the Hawaiian tradition." A regal tilt of her head indicated the lei he wore. "I wish that you should also feel welcome in the Japanese way. Please come in, Wesley. Hiroshi will see to your luggage when he returns."

She moved gracefully into the foyer. "Please," she said, indicating that he should remove his shoes here. She looked pointedly at her granddaughter, obviously expecting her to perform this service for their guest.

Lani looked away, pretending she hadn't noticed. She had, on countless occasions, knelt to remove her father's shoes, or her grandmother's, or even Dave Yamazaki's. *But I'll be damned if I'll kneel in front of Wes Adams,* she thought vehemently, sitting down on a lacquered bench to take off her Topsiders. The man would take it entirely the wrong way. She straightened, her shoes in one hand, and looked up—directly into Wes's amused blue eyes.

Fomi, the housekeeper, was kneeling at his feet—*where you should be*, his teasing eyes said—with a pair of backless slippers in her hands. His shoes sat, side-by-side, near her knees. Still holding Lani's gaze, Wes lifted each foot in turn as Fomi slid the house shoes on.

"*Arigato gozaimasu*," he thanked her in faultless Japanese, giving her such a brilliant smile that Fomi hid, giggling, behind her hands, and scurried off in the direction of the kitchen.

"Lani will show you to your room, Wesley. The *furo* is in readiness should you wish to use it," Sumiko said, referring to the communal bath. "Please do not feel rushed, we will dine when you are ready." She bowed again and turned gracefully to follow her housekeeper.

"'We will dine when you are ready,'" Lani mimicked her grandmother good-naturedly. "Gran never could resist a pretty face."

"Meaning me?" Wes grinned at her.

"Meaning you." She gave him a considering look. "You look a lot like your Uncle Gerard, which would make her even worse." She turned into the hallway to their left. "The bedrooms are this way," she said over her shoulder. "They're furnished Japanese fashion. Which means you sleep on quilted mattresses—*futon*—on the floor. They each have their own American-style bath, though, with a shower." She slid open a door. "This is the *furo*, the Japanese soaking tub Gran spoke of. Do you know the routine?"

"I've spent some time in the Orient."

"Good, then you know the do's and don'ts." She paused before the next door. "This is your room while you're here. Fomi will have laid out a *yukata*—a sort of cotton robe—if you'd like to get comfortable for dinner. If you need anything else, just call."

Wes reached out and grabbed her wrist lightly, pulling her around to face him as she turned to go. He grinned wickedly before he spoke. "Do you come in and share the *furo* with me?"

Lani raised a slender hand to his chest to steady herself as he spun her around. It was warm and hard under her fingers. Solid as a rock. "Not a chance," she said lightly, struggling to keep her breathing calm and even as images of Wes, naked and wet, tumbled crazily through her mind. She pulled her wrist from his grasp and backed away, reaching behind her for the door of her own room. "I'll send Fomi in to scrub your back if you like," she said, and disappeared behind a sliding panel.

Wes stood where he was for a few moments longer, staring at the closed door. So she'd send Fomi in to him, would she? Well, he didn't want Fomi. He wanted Lani. He'd be more than happy to have *her* scrub his back, for a start. And then . . . His eyes glazed over for a second as he envisioned all the possibilities of sharing a bath with the deliciously diminutive Ms Lani MacPherson. Then he grinned wolfishly, shaking his head to clear it, and opened the sliding panel to his room.

BEHIND HER BEDROOM DOOR Lani stood with flushed cheeks, silently cursing Wes for the unexpected, unwanted—*totally unwanted,* she assured herself—feelings he had aroused in her. She didn't have time for this! Especially not with her grandmother's hand-picked henchman. "Hell," she said aloud, shaking her head to dispel the ridiculous images that formed in her mind at the mere thought of the man.

She moved to her lacquered dresser and poured herself a cup of tea from the tiny teapot kept warm under a quilted tea cozy. A cup of hot green tea, she thought, a few minutes' quite reflection and she would put him and his wicked pirate's smile completely out of her mind.

"I hope," she muttered, sinking down into the flowered cushions of a rattan chair with the teacup in her hand. Lifting her feet to the matching footstool, she leaned her head back and gazed out onto the garden through the open glass doors in front of her. *Concentrate on the garden*, she told herself. *Think peaceful thoughts.*

The garden was her grandmother's pride and joy, full of bright Hawaiian flowers; fragrant jasmine, paper-white narcissus, hibiscus, flaming Bird of Paradise, myriad orchids and spicy Hawaiian ginger. That's what the lei she had given Wes was made of, she mused. Ginger. The tiny cinnamon-colored flowers had looked especially delicate around his strong neck, their spicy scent doubly sweet when contrasted with the faintly citrusy after-shave he wore.

Lani gave herself a mental shake. *Peaceful thoughts*, she reminded herself sternly. *Think peaceful thoughts. Think about the garden.*

Her eyes wandered over the banana trees along the back fence and the two cherry trees near the *koi* pond. Painted glass wind chimes hung among the branches, their faint music tinkling through the house and garden with every soft breath of air.

Lani sighed. It was so beautiful, so peaceful. She wondered if Wes was appreciating the identical view from the room next to hers. If he—

"Damn!" she said aloud. Her feet hit the floor with a thud and she stood up, sloshing tea over the back of her hand. "Damn," she said again, all but slamming the cup down on top of her dresser. A framed eight-by-ten color glossy trembled slightly. Absently Lani reached out to steady it, then checked, and picked it up instead.

She looked down into the smiling faces of her parents on their wedding day. Her father was handsome and serious in a conventional blue suit, his flaming red hair slicked down, his mustache bushy. Her mother was exotic and doll-like in her rainbow-colored kimono and elaborate wedding head-dress. It was her father's face Lani stared at; she had very little memory of the mother who had died in a boating ac-cident when Lani was four.

"Well, Pop, whad'a'ya think?" she said to the picture. Si-lence was her only answer. "I could be in real trouble here, Pop," she told him. "Real trouble." Her father continued to smile up at her. Lani sighed and sat the picture back on her dresser. It was time she got dressed for dinner anyway, she told herself, turning toward her closet.

She supposed, judging from her grandmother's formal attire, that she was expected to appear in a kimono for din-ner. She had several to choose from and usually enjoyed wearing them. But not tonight. She knew full well how she looked in a kimono; delicate and feminine and as helpless as a painted doll. And tonight she didn't want to look help-less, not in front of Wes Adams. Or her grandmother, if it came to that. She wanted to look strong and liberated and well able to run a business on her own. Not an easy impres-sion to give when you were wrapped in yards of heavy silk and forced to take tiny mincing steps.

For a moment she considered putting on one of her West-ern-style dresses or, perhaps, a Hawaiian *pareau*. But only for a moment. They would be eating Japanese-style to-night; they always did when they had company. Western dinner dresses weren't made for kneeling and a *pareau*—a graceful, strapless dress that tied above the bosom—was even more rife with suggestion than a kimono. Besides, her grandmother had obviously gone to a lot of trouble to make Wes's first evening with them special. She would be hurt if Lani did anything to spoil it.

The kimono Lani selected was made of a heavy lavender silk, lavishly embroidered on the flowing sleeves and around the lower edge of the floor-length skirt in lighter and darker shades of lavender and purple. The stiff brocade obi wrapped snugly around her waist, forming a wide, flat bow in back. Like Sumiko, she wore *tabi*, ankle socks split for thongs, and the backless, thonged sandals called zori.

She fastened lavender jade ovals in the lobes of her ears, then made up her eyes quickly, adding to and intensifying the light makeup she had put on that morning. A dusting of blusher on her cheeks, a dab of clear gloss on her lips, and she was ready. The face that stared back at her from the mirror was one of exotic beauty, much like one of the painted geishas that hung in the living room. All exotic black eyes and shiny black hair with no hint of the red highlights so apparent in the sun. Lani made a face at herself, sticking out her tongue, and ran a hand through the silk fringe of her hair, pushing the slanting bangs off her forehead. The geisha was gone, replaced by a thoroughly modern young woman dressed up in costume.

"Well," she said to her reflection. "Gran will be pleased."

She rose gracefully from her dressing table and exited her room through the glass doors to the garden, taking the tiny mincing steps demanded by the kimono. She tried not to think of Wes's reaction when he saw her decked out like a delicate Japanese doll.

3

BOTH WES AND HER GRANDMOTHER were on the lanai when
Lani made her appearance. Seated companionably side by
side on a cushioned rattan sofa under the dappled shade of
the latticed roof, they were carrying on a low-voiced conversation in a mixture of Japanese and English.

Sumiko sat daintily upright, her rigid back never touching the flowered cushion behind her, her hands folded
gracefully on her lap. She had a look of rapt attention on
her face as she listened to Wes. Her slight nods of agreement set her hair ornaments swaying gently with a faint
tinkling sound.

No man could fail to be flattered by such undivided attention, thought Lani as she made her slow, mincing way
across the lawn. The air of serene and gentle calm that surrounded Sumiko would soothe even the most savage beast
and Wes, it seemed, was no exception.

He was leaning back against the cushions, entirely at his
ease, one muscular forearm resting on the back of the sofa
behind Sumiko, the other hand describing something in the
air before him as he talked. A tall, frosty glass sat on a glass-
topped table within easy reach. A small platter of beautifully arranged hors d'oeuvres sat beside it.

He had changed clothes, taking advantage of the comfortable navy batik *yukata* that Fomi had laid out for him,
and was wearing the knee-length, robelike garment over
pale gray slacks with a careless elegance that suggested fa-
miliarity with Oriental dress. It was loosely crossed in front

and belted with a navy sash, its V-neck leaving a tempting wedge of his tanned chest bare. Crinkly sun-kissed hair dusted the exposed skin.

The man, Lani decided sourly, looked practically edible.

He finished his story to Sumiko, leaning forward for his drink just as Lani reached the bottom step of the lanai. Seeing her, he rose swiftly—like a pirate leaping to the quarterdeck, Lani thought—and stepped around the low glass table to the edge of the lanai, his hand extended to help her up the steps. Without thinking, Lani lifted the long skirt of her kimono in one hand and placed the other one in his.

Instantly that same tingling spark that she had felt earlier shot through her. Her eyes flared wide for just a second. Her fingers jumped as if she meant to pull away. But she quelled the impulse almost immediately, instinctively knowing that to yank her hand from his would only serve to show him—and her grandmother—just how he affected her. Instead, eyes demurely lowered, she let him lead her to the rattan chair across from her grandmother, hoping that she hadn't given herself away.

He seated her almost ceremoniously; arranging a small pillow behind her back, handing her the iced drink that Fomi stood holding on a tray before she could reach for it herself. She accepted it with a low murmur of thanks and then, steeling herself, she lifted her eyes to his.

She'd given herself away after all, she thought, staring up at him. But he'd given himself away, as well. There was something in his eyes as he returned her steady gaze. Something that said he was as affected as she was by the simple touch of palm to palm.

But it couldn't be, she thought then. Because she didn't *want* it to be. She didn't want him to be attracted to her any more than she wanted to be attracted to him. It would complicate things too much. And things were complicated enough already.

She shook her head slightly, almost imperceptibly, denying the thought, the feeling, as she sat there, still as a statue, her eyes locked with his. They held the stare for a moment longer, a heartbeat's worth of time that seemed to stretch for aeons. Staring, searching for...something. And then a low-voiced question from her grandmother took his attention away.

"Pardon?" he said, almost groggily, turning from Lani to look at Sumiko. There was that feeling again, he thought, that sizzle of attraction that felt more and more like a terminal case of lust. "I'm sorry, I didn't hear what you said, Mrs. Walsh-san."

Released from his spell, Lani lowered her eyes to her lap again. Both hands were clutched tightly around the glass he had handed her. Deliberately she relaxed her fingers and set the untasted drink on the table in front of her.

This is ridiculous, she scolded herself, folding her hands together in her lap again. *Ridiculous! I only met the man a few hours ago. He can't possibly have gotten under my skin so fast. He can't have—*

It's the kimono, she decided then, seeking a reason for her unwanted response to Wes. A kimono always made her feel soft and feminine and receptive. And it always seemed to make men feel more like, well, men. That was it. Hadn't she told herself exactly that when she was putting the damn thing on? But you weren't wearing a kimono earlier, a little voice said inside her head. Not at the side of the road when he'd turned her all tingly with a look. Not in the hallway when he'd touched her. Both those times he had made her feel something, she thought, shying away from giving that something a label. And he'd done it with little more than a

glance from those pirate's eyes of his, with just the barest
touch of his hand. Imagine what would happen if he—

Lani gave herself a mental shake and scowled at her
hands, appalled at the direction her thoughts were taking.
He's the enemy, she reminded herself, forgetting that she had
already decided that he really wasn't. She couldn't let mere
physical attraction make her forget that. That's just what
her grandmother was counting on.

Well, Gran, she thought, focusing on her more familiar
and far less formidable opponent, *you're one crafty old
lady, but I'm your granddaughter and Thomas Mac-
Pherson's daughter, so that makes us just about even. And
no good-looking lawyer from the mainland is going to finagle his way around me.* She picked up her glass and raised
it slightly in a silent toast. *Let the battle begin,* she thought,
and smiled at herself for her dramatics.

Wes caught her gesture with the glass and the small, cat-
like smile that accompanied it. His right eyebrow slid up
inquiringly. But Lani only smiled more sweetly, giving him
her best inscrutable face, and rose gracefully, as her grandmother had taught her, to answer Fomi's summons for dinner.

She's up to something, Wes thought, staring at her
straight slender back under the lavender silk of the kimono
as he followed her into the house. He couldn't wait to find
out what it was.

THE LOW, lacquered dining-room table had been beautifully set in the best of both American and Japanese tradition. An exquisite bonsai made of pale green jade served as
a centerpiece. Two tiny golden deer stood under its gleaming branches and a single white china Tiare blossom rested
at its base. The china was Sumiko's best, made of fine white
porcelain with hand-painted red, green and gold dragons

chasing each other around the rim. The glass chopstick rests were fashioned to resemble tiny *koi* or goldfish. The chopsticks were ivory. Steaming bowls of hot clear broth garnished with sliced bamboo shoots and a single curl of lemon peel waited at each place, inviting them to begin the feast.

Sumiko indicated that Wes, as the honored guest, should sit at the head of the table. She and Lani knelt on the cushions at either side of him. Without a word, Lani rose to her knees to pour fragrant green tea for each of them before offering sake, a warm rice wine. At Wes's nod, she filled his sake cup and sank back down on her cushion again, resting lightly on her heels, her back ramrod straight, her hands folded on her lap, waiting for Wes to begin eating.

Her actions were unthinking, automatic. Since childhood she had been taught by Sumiko the traditional and gracious way to serve a guest and her actions would have been the same regardless of who sat at the head of the table. And, now, no matter how galling it was to appear so submissive before Wes, her sense of duty to her grandmother kept her silent. Sumiko would have been shamed had her granddaughter done otherwise.

But after today, Lani reminded herself, frowning at Wes as he grinned at her over the sake cup, he would no longer have honored-guest status and she could be as unpleasant as she pleased. At least when Sumiko wasn't looking.

Putting down his sake, Wes tasted the steaming broth before him. Smacking his lips loudly, as politeness demanded, he declared to the hovering Fomi that it was the best he'd ever tasted. Fomi, in turn, denied that it was fit to eat, apologized for the humbleness of the dish and, custom satisfied, retired to the kitchen to begin the next course.

"I can't decide," Wes said, "whether I like your little geisha face better or the hot-tempered women's libber that rescued me."

"Lani was impolite?" asked Sumiko before Lani could say anything.

"No, not impolite. Let's say—" his blue eyes twinkled at Lani for a moment, anticipating the fireworks that were sure to follow his words "—outspoken," he said, and grinned at her.

Lani's eyes flashed a warning.

Wes ignored it. "She seems to think I'm here at your request to part her from her, ah, inheritance." His grin got wider. More devilish. "And she went to great pains to assure me that such a thing isn't possible."

Sumiko sighed delicately. "My granddaughter has always been an impulsive child," she said in her low, musical voice, completely disregarding the fact that the said "child" was twenty-five years old. "At present we are in disagreement over her wish to run her father's business." The look she turned on Lani was gently censoring. "Apparently she credits me with a deviousness I do not possess."

"Oh, Lani never said you were—" Wes began.

"Lani would like to say," Lani said, with more patience than she was feeling, "that she doesn't like being talked about as if she wasn't here. And the term isn't women's libber." She flashed a quick, narrowed-eyed look at Wes. "It's feminist."

Wes inclined his head slightly, graciously acknowledging the point. "Again, I stand corrected, Ms MacPherson."

Lani inclined her head just as graciously, annoyed by but ignoring the slight emphasis he had placed on the word Ms.

"Have you done something to your eyes?" he asked then, as if he wasn't introducing a whole new topic of conversation.

Lani blinked. "My eyes?"

"Yes." He reached out and touched her eyelid. Lani forced herself not to flinch away from the heat that sizzled through

her at his light touch. "They look more Oriental somehow," he said. "Exotic." His hand dropped back to the table. "Very becoming."

"Thank you," she said stiffly. What else could she say?
Don't touch me, it makes me crazy? Keep your hands to
yourself or I'll chop 'em off at the wrists? That's what she'd
like to say but— "I'm sorry, Gran, were you talking to me?"

Sumiko merely lifted her eyes to the door leading into the
kitchen; Fomi was bringing out another platter.

"Ah, Fomi-san," Wes said as the housekeeper set the
platter of thinly sliced raw fish on the table. "How did you
know sashimi was my favorite Japanese dish?"

Fomi giggled and blushed as she bowed herself out of the
room.

Under her grandmother's watchful eye, Lani again rose
to her knees to serve Wes. She transferred some fish to his
plate with a pair of chopsticks, then offered him his choice
of either soy sauce or spicy green horseradish to dip it in.
All her movements were studied and graceful, her eyes
lowered as befit a well-brought-up Japanese woman. And
then Sumiko nodded, pleased with Lani's behavior, and
looked down at her plate.

Lani's black eyes lifted to Wes's, daggers in their obsidian
depths. "I hope it chokes you," she mouthed distinctly, before smiling sweetly and sinking back on her heels.

Wes grinned. His laughing, devil-may-care pirate's grin,
the one that invited her to laugh with him. And sitting there,
somewhere between anger, excitement and unwilling
amusement, she almost did.

"Gerard is well?" Sumiko asked then, saving her granddaughter from that folly.

Lani looked down at her plate, quickly reaching to serve
herself a portion of sashimi, glad to have her grandmother
take his attention from her.

"Yes, Gerard is fine. As always," Wes said, turning toward Sumiko. "He sends his love."

"As I send him mine," Sumiko said quietly.

Wes flicked a quick glance at Lani. He found her eyes waiting. They smiled at each other, a quick, secret smile. Family legend had it that Gerard Adams had been in love with Sumiko since the minute Edward Walsh had introduced his future bride to his best man. It was common knowledge that he'd proposed to her exactly a year after his best friend's death, and that he continued to propose to her every year since then. What the inscrutable Sumiko felt about his devotion, nobody knew. And nobody had ever dared to ask.

"He briefed me on the problem you're having at Walsh Imports," Wes said to Sumiko when Lani looked back at her plate. "But he said you'd fill me in on the details."

"Yes, Gran," Lani said coaxingly, her voice almost sugary sweet. "Fill us in on the details." Not for a minute did she believe there was any kind of real problem at Walsh Imports.

"It is as I told Gerard over the telephone," Sumiko said. "There has been a theft at Walsh Imports and—"

"A theft!" Lani exclaimed. This was the first she'd heard about any theft! "When? Who? Why didn't you tell me?" she demanded of her grandmother.

Sumiko motioned her to silence. "I saw no need, Granddaughter. It was a small theft. Only a few pieces were taken and they have been returned. So I thought that would be the end of it."

"But it wasn't," Wes said.

"No. The culprit was a young relative of David Yamazaki's. The son of his second cousin, I believe. The boy has been dismissed, of course. And since the merchandise has been returned, no charges have been brought against him."

Sumiko sighed. "He is very young and I believe he has learned his lesson from this."

"Then everything's settled," Lani said, rising up to her knees a little. "So why—"

Sumiko frowned and held up her hand for silence. Lani immediately subsided, eyes downcast, hands folded in her lap in an attitude of respectful submission. She was acutely aware of Wes's interested attention. Her immediate obedience to Sumiko's gesture must seem greatly at odds with her loudly proclaimed feminist viewpoint. Her only defense was that she'd been conditioned. Since childhood her grandmother's raised hand had always had the power to quell any outburst on Lani's part, even when the shouted threats and blustering of her giant, red-haired father had had no effect.

"David feels dishonored," Sumiko continued when she was satisfied that Lani wouldn't interrupt again. "He is deeply shamed by the action of his young relative and he was prepared to submit his resignation. Walsh Imports cannot afford to lose such a valued and trusted employee, and I believe I have prevailed upon him to stay. But he wished to have a complete inventory taken, by someone other than himself or his staff, and the records carefully checked so that we may be assured that he has not cheated our family also."

Wow, thought Lani inadequately. There really was a problem for Walsh Imports, and not a little one, either. Walsh Imports couldn't afford to lose Dave Yamazaki. Dave *was* Walsh Imports and had been since her grandfather's death twelve years ago. There was no one in the Islands more knowledgeable about Japanese antiques, or more loyal.

So there was good reason for Wes to be in Hawaii. A very good reason.

"Do you believe Dave's story?" he said to Sumiko, his blue eyes deadly serious for once.

Sumiko nodded serenely. "Of course," she said. "Completely. You do not?"

"I don't know him well enough to believe or disbelieve," he answered. "But I needed to know what you thought." He leaned back a little to allow Fomi to remove the nearly empty platter of sashimi. "So it appears to be only a matter of getting that inventory taken and going over the books, then?"

Sumiko nodded.

"And you're sure that will satisfy Mr. Yamazaki's need to save face?"

Sumiko nodded again. "Yes."

"Good. Then let's leave any more discussion of business until after dinner." He smiled up at the housekeeper as she placed another laden platter on the table in front of him. "Or Fomi will begin to think I don't like her cooking."

4

LANI OPENED HER EYES suddenly, not sure what had awakened her. She lay on her stomach, her face all but buried in the pillow, listening. The darkness was all around, the quiet of the night seeming to cushion her from the outside world. Her bed was still, not rocking as it would be if a boat had cruised through the harbor. No light, no sound, no movement, nothing that would account for her abrupt awakening from a sound sleep.

And then she remembered. She wasn't bunked down in the berth on one of her boats as she was so often these days because she had worked late. She was home. It was probably the very lack of sound and movement that had brought her awake.

She levered herself up onto an elbow, squinting at the clock on the shelf above her bed of *futons* on the floor. Three forty-five. Nowhere near time to get up. She dropped her head back to the pillow with a groan, burrowing into it like a small animal searching for cover, and closed her eyes, willing herself back to sleep.

But it was no use. She was wide awake. Sighing, she rolled over to her side, punching her pillow into a more comfortable position beneath her head, and gazed out the partially open glass doors to the garden.

The moon was almost full, its mystical glow lighting up the garden like a hazy spotlight. From where she lay, Lani could see its soft reflection on the *koi* pond and the dark, secret shadows cast under the banana trees over by the back fence. A night breeze stirred the air, setting the wind chimes to singing softly, sending a sprinkle of cherry blossoms fluttering to the lawn. The gauzy curtains at the glass doors of her bedroom billowed and ebbed, carrying with them the heady scent of night-blooming jasmine and the faint tanginess of the surrounding sea. Lani pushed her cover off restlessly, letting the warm air caress her bare legs, and rolled over again, onto her back this time, and folded her arms under her head.

The thought of Wes came, unbidden, to her mind as she lay there in her bed and stared up at the ceiling.

Curse and rot him, she thought, calling up her father's favorite expletive. It was his fault she couldn't sleep. His and that wily, manipulating, scheming grandmother of hers. Not that she still believed that Wes had any part in her grandmother's hare-brained matchmaking scheme. She had absolved him of all involvement in it when she learned about the very real problem at Walsh Imports. But he didn't really need to be in on the scheme. Sumiko could use him as a diversion with or without his overt cooperation.

And she did. Oh, yes, she did.

Lani had sat all through dinner and the polite conversation afterward, doing her best to ignore all the pleased, pointed looks that Sumiko sent her way.

Is he not cultured? her eyes said when Wes made some salient point about the small jade bonsai that decorated the table. He had several like it in his collection, he'd said, as well as a reproduction of the tall Japanese urn that stood in a corner of the dining room. "Seventeenth century, isn't it?" he'd added, then proceeded to discuss some of the various techniques used to date such antiques, a process which obviously fascinated him.

Is he not educated? Sumiko communicated when he made them see a precise point of law, punctuating his sentences with quick, controlled jabs in the air. "Of course, my field's corporate law, not criminal, but the concept's the same," he'd said modestly. Which, Lani noted dryly, only drove him up another notch in Sumiko's estimation. Both for his modesty and the fact that he dealt in the more refined area of corporate law as opposed to associating with the criminal element.

Is he not sensitive? the elderly Japanese woman demanded silently when Wes waxed poetic about the sunrise as seen from the summit of Japan's Mount Norikura, comparing it to the sight of the dawn breaking over a snow-capped peak of the Sierras.

And then he mentioned his love of sailing and the sleek little sloop he kept harbored in San Francisco Bay. "I've always dreamed of taking some time off and sailing around the world," he said, not mentioning that he was about to make that dream come true.

Sumiko turned her eyes to her granddaughter again. *Does he not share your interests?* they asked. *Is he not perfect for you in every way?*

Lani had looked down at her hands at that and wished the evening were over. Because he was just about perfect, damn him, and if she were looking for a husband or a serious relationship he might well be a likely candidate. But she wasn't looking, so it was a moot point.

She was still telling herself that when he'd walked across the garden with her later, matching his long, rolling stride to her more restricted steps, making her aware, in a very elemental way, of his size and strength and maleness. Knowing how it would affect her, she had refused the offer of his arm as they strolled across the lawn, but he was still close enough for her to smell the faint citrusy scent of his aftershave. It was pleasantly mixed with the scent of sake and his own unique male scent. It had warmed her almost as much as his touch had done and she'd had to stop herself from leaning closer and inhaling him.

He left her outside her bedroom door with a brief "G'night, Ms MacPherson," and a look that suggested that he might like to be going into her bedroom with her, if only they were alone in the big house. She'd found herself wishing that they were.

"Oh, hell! Enough of this rot!" Lani jerked upright in the middle of the *futons,* as if action could dispel her wayward thoughts, and got to her feet.

Since sleep seemed impossible and she didn't like the direction her solitary thoughts were taking, she decided that she might as well get something to eat. Something sweet, with a glass of milk and a dull book would either put her back to sleep or, at the very least, keep her mind from wandering dangerously until it was time to get up.

She slipped a short matching robe over her cream-colored satin tap pants and camisole and, disregarding her slippers, made her way silently from her room and across the garden, heading for the kitchen on the other side of the U-shaped house.

The grass was dewy, wet but not cold against her bare feet. The air was soft and warm, the scent of flowers and the sea stronger than it had been in her room. By force of habit, she paused beside the *koi* pond for a moment to count the fish. There were seven. A family tradition had been started when, as a child, her mother had declared that you got one wish for each fish in the pond.

"Let me make a success of Sail Away," Lani began, wishing on the first fish. "Let me—" She stopped, laughing softly to herself, and turned away from the pond. All of her wishes were for the success of Sail Away. She wasn't sure if the magic would work if you used all your wishes on one thing.

Leaving a trail of small wet footprints across the lanai, she entered the open kitchen doors. The moon was so bright, even inside, that she didn't need to turn on any lights. She opened the refrigerator door, shivering slightly as the cold air hit her bare arms and legs. A large portion of one of Fomi's coconut cream pies sat on the second shelf. Lani's mouth began to water; Fomi made the best coconut cream pies in the world.

Telling herself that she'd atone for pigging out tomorrow, Lani found a small bamboo tray and set the piece of pie on it, then poured herself a glass of milk. Closing the refrigerator door with her foot, the tray balanced in both hands, she spied the fruit bowl. Giving in to temptation, she shifted the tray to one hip and reached out, adding an orange and small cluster of grapes to her booty, and turned toward the kitchen door, intending to take her midnight feast to her room. She had just reached the edge of the lanai when a voice from the darkness behind her caused her to pause in midstep.

"Got enough there for two?"

Lani turned slowly, mindful of her laden tray, and peered into the shadows cast by the slanting roof of the lanai. She couldn't see anyone until the glowing end of a cheroot gave away his position.

"Wes?" she said, squinting to find him in the shadows. There was no answer. Little shivers of anticipation and unwilling excitement raced up her spine. "Wes, I know that's you," she said sharply, telling herself that it was annoyance and nothing else that had caused her heart to suddenly beat faster. "Come out here where I can see you."

Her answer was a deep, throaty laugh as Wes pushed himself away from the wall. He crushed out his cheroot in an ashtray that Sumiko had ordered to be placed on one of the glass-topped tables, and moved out into the moonlight. "Not so loud, Moonmaid. You'll wake the whole house."

He came toward her slowly, almost warily, like a pirate circling an unfamiliar opponent. He was shirtless and barefoot, wearing only a pair of faded jeans. The moonlight glinted off the fuzzy mat of his curling chest hairs, making them glimmer like gold in the wavering shadows. His bare shoulders looked bigger and broader than they had under his clothes. The rounded muscles flexed under his skin, flowing into the longer muscles of his arms and the smooth, hard mounds of his pectorals, stretching down over his lean ribs to the drum-tight flatness of his belly.

He looked, she thought, staring at him dry-mouthed, like nothing so much as a pirate captain prowling the deck, made restless by the tropical night. All he lacked was an eye patch, a gold earring and a captive maiden by his side. Or, perhaps his captive had managed to lock him out of his cabin and that's why he was pacing the deck by himself. Maybe—

"You startled me," Lani hissed, annoyed at the nonsensical direction of her thoughts. *Pirates and captive maidens, indeed!* What was the matter with her?

"I'm sorry," Wes said, not looking sorry at all. His eyes roamed over her face, touching her eyes, lingering over her lips, trailing down the delicate line of her jaw, to her rounded, bite-sized chin.

He'd been awake for an hour or more, sitting out on the lanai, smoking and thinking about her, his eyes on the billowing curtains at the door of her bedroom. Knowing it was open, he wondered what would happen if he took advantage of the unintentional invitation and crawled into the *futon* beside her.

And then, as if he'd conjured her up out of wishes and dreams, she appeared. Wrapped in something short and silky, her hair inky black in the moonlight, she came creeping out of her room, tiptoeing across the garden, as seemingly insubstantial as a moonbeam. He'd watched her pause beside the *koi* pond for a moment, heard her laugh softly as if one of the fish had said something funny. It wasn't until he smelled the faint scent of sandalwood and roses as she walked by him on her way into the kitchen that he'd known for sure she was real and not a product of wishful thinking. Insubstantial moonbeams didn't smell that good.

When she'd come out again, carrying the tray, he'd considered sitting silently and letting her return, unmolested, to her room. She was, after all, the granddaughter of a valued friend and a long-time client of his uncle's. She had made her disinclination to get involved very clear. And he was all set to sail off into the sunset when he'd taken care of the inventory at Walsh Imports. Or he would be, when he'd found a boat. So, anyway you looked at it, he told himself, it wouldn't be wise to start something. Even if her grandmother did seem to have given her unspoken approval. Although Sumiko's approval probably didn't extend to his seducing her only grandchild.

He'd let her get all the way to the edge of the lanai before he'd come to his feet and called to her. The action surprised him almost as much as it did her; he really hadn't meant to.

"What have you got there?" he said then, forcing himself to speak calmly. His insides were coiling with the same emotion that had taken hold of him when she'd lifted the lei over her head to show him the logo on her T-shirt. Rampant lust, he told himself, wondering if that's really all it was.

Lani had to clear her throat before she could answer him; he was standing so close, practically looming over her, that speaking was difficult. "A snack." She held the tray a little higher as if to draw his attention to it. Or as if she were trying to protect herself from his heated gaze.

He glanced down at the tray. What he saw there made him laugh softly, easing the tension with which he had been holding himself. "Good Lord, you weren't planning to eat all that?" he said in disbelief. "There's enough there for three people."

Lani looked down at the tray, too. Her soft embarrassed laugh echoed his. "I guess my eyes are bigger than my stomach. Want to share?" Good manners, she told herself, were all that had made her ask.

Wes nodded and stepped back, allowing Lani to place the tray on one of the glass-topped tables.

"We'll need another fork," she said nervously, looking at the tray. "And plates. I'll get them." She returned in a few minutes with the needed utensils and another glass of milk, her nerves no more settled than before the few minutes it had taken her to find them. "Can't eat Fomi's coconut cream pie without milk," she said as she set the glass down and proceeded to divide the pie.

She handed Wes his share, being careful that her fingers didn't touch his, then curled up in a lounge chair opposite him. "Couldn't you sleep?" she asked, deliberately casual, trying to pretend that there was nothing unsettling about sitting out on the lanai in the moonlight, sharing pie with a half-dressed man.

He shook his head and swallowed a mouthful of pie. "Time difference. It's already morning for me." And it was, too, but that wasn't the reason he couldn't sleep. He forked up another bite of pie. "Great pie," he said, washing it down with a sip of milk. The glass clicked against the table as he set it down. "How about you, Moonmaid, why couldn't you sleep?"

"Something woke me. Hunger pangs, I guess," she lied, making designs in the whipped cream topping of her pie with the tines of her fork. "I couldn't drop back off."

Wes nodded, accepting that. Another silent moment passed, and then another as they both pretended absorbed interest in the pie on their plates.

"Great pie," Wes said again, although he couldn't have said what kind it was.

"Yes, it is," Lani agreed. "Why did you call me 'Moon-maid'?" she asked, almost blurting it out.

"Did I?"

"Twice."

"Well, I guess because that's what you looked like coming across the garden in the moonlight. All that shadowy tanned skin and dark hair and your nightgown—or whatever you call that scrap you're wearing—the color of moonbeams wrapped around you. Very otherworldly."

Lani looked down at herself with dismay, suddenly aware of her lack of proper dress. The thin satiny robe fell open around her, revealing the wide-legged tap pants and cami-sole top she'd worn to sleep in. The entire length of her long, tanned legs and a good deal of her fragile upper chest was left bare to his gaze. Instinctively she tucked her feet a little farther under her, her free hand rearranging the front of her robe so that it covered more of her.

"Isn't that a little silly?" Wes said.

Lani looked up to find him eyeing her with amusement, his right eyebrow quirked mockingly. Flushing, she smoothed her lapel, then dropped her hand to her lap.

"I'm sure you wear much less than that at the beach in full view of hundreds of people."

"This isn't the beach," she reminded him.

"No, but I assure you, you're quite decently covered." And then, suddenly, he gave her that wicked pirate's grin of his that left her so breathless. "It's a shame to cover a body like that anyway."

Pleased and embarrassed and looking anywhere but at him, Lani leaned forward to put her uneaten pie on the table. "So, ah, tell me about the sailboat you have anchored in San Francisco," she said nervously, reaching for the orange on the tray. "You said it was a sloop?" She rolled the fruit between her hands as she spoke, loosening the skin before peeling it.

"A twenty-six-foot Columbia. The *Whodunit*."

Her hands stilled on the orange. "The *Whodunit*." She said the name slowly, testing the sound of it. "Very law-yerly," she approved, trying to dig her thumb into the tough skin of the fruit. "Do you sail her often?"

"As often as I can—a couple of weekends a month if I'm lucky." His mouth twisted up in a grimace. "Which, lately, I haven't been. Here, give me that." He took the orange out of her hand, separated a strip of the peel from the pulp, and handed it back to her.

"Thanks."

He nodded. "It seems as if the whole country has gone crazy with lawsuits these days," he went on. "So I've been busier than usual, trying to get as many cases as possible cleared up before I take my leave."

"Leave?" she said, handing him half of the peeled orange.

He accepted it absently. "I'm taking a year's leave from the firm." He didn't want to go into the why of it. That why—a vague dissatisfaction with what he'd spent the past ten years of his life doing—sounded self-indulgent, even to him. "I'm planning to do some blue water sailing." He popped a slice of orange into his mouth. "Maybe only as far as from here to Tahiti. Maybe as far as the coast of Africa." He shrugged, the muscles of his broad shoulders rippling with the movement. "Maybe all the way around the world. I haven't really decided."

"On the *Whodunit*?"

He shook his head, pausing to swallow another slice of orange before answering. "I've been looking around for another boat to buy. Something larger. With more equipment. Some state-of-the-art navigational gear. A single band radio. That kind of thing."

"Well, you've come to the right place. Hawaii's a buyer's market," Lani said knowledgeably, at ease with a subject she knew inside out. "There are a couple of boats that might interest you down at Ala Wai Harbor. If you want to stop by my office one afternoon before you go back to San Francisco, I'd be happy to introduce you to the owners."

"I'd appreciate that." His half of the orange gone, he wiped his sticky hands on his jeans. "I wouldn't mind getting in an afternoon of sailing in one of your boats, either," he hinted, his eyes holding a glimmer of that little-boy look she found so appealing.

Lani smiled. "Sure. Let me know when and I can book one of the sailboats for an afternoon. There are some beautiful beaches on Oahu that are accessible only by boat," she told him. "We could get Fomi to make us a picnic and make a day of it, if you like."

"I like."

"It's a date then." She smiled, always happy to share something she loved so much with someone she— She veered away from completing the thought. Thoughts like that were dangerous. "So." She cast around for another topic of conversation. "Then I guess you're not here just to clear up the inventory problem at Walsh Imports after all."

He grinned at her, his wicked pirate's grin. "I never said I was."

That grin disconcerted her. "No, I guess you didn't." Head down, she concentrated on separating a section of orange from its neighbor. "So," she said again, "how long will it take you to go over Dave's books and complete the inventory at Walsh Imports?"

Unaccountably, he took offense at that; after the past few minutes of companionable conversation, it felt as if she were trying to get rid of him. "You mean how long will I be providing you with a diversion?"

She brought her head up sharply and met his eyes. She hadn't meant anything specific by her question but he seemed to be challenging her in some way, or teasing her, maybe. She couldn't read the expression in his eyes. Leaning forward, she put the uneaten portion of her orange back on the tray, telling herself that she didn't want to read it. "I didn't mean it like that," she said, shrugging. "I was just making conversation. But since you brought it up—" She leveled a look at him. "When will you be leaving?"

"What difference does it make to you?" For some reason he suddenly wanted to rile her. "I'm here at your grandmother's request, on your grandmother's business, not yours."

"Yes! And until you're gone, I can expect no peace from her on the subject of Sail Away."

"I thought we'd agreed that I have nothing to do with her scheme."

"*We* may have. *She* hasn't. And she won't. As long as you're here and she thinks there's a chance that I might, ah . . ." She stumbled over the words, knowing what she wanted to say but not exactly how to say it without embarrassing herself. "Might . . ."

"Yes?" Wes said, all innocence. He knew what she was trying so hard to avoid saying. He wanted her to say it. "You might what?"

Lani's eyes narrowed. "You know *what*." She brought her feet out from under her, placing them flat on the lanai floor, and leaned forward, an earnest expression on her face. "As long as you're here, Gran will keep at me—and you, too, you know—thinking if I just, ah, if I just fell for you," she said it quickly, her eyes skittering away from his, "that I'd forget all this 'foolishness about running Sail Away.' But if you leave without that happening, I think she might finally come to realize that I'm not going to give up Sail Away under *any* circumstances. As long as you're here, though, she'll keep thinking that there's a chance her crazy scheme is going to work." Her eyes met his again, direct and unwavering. "And she'll make both our lives miserable while she's at it," she warned. "You can count on it."

Wes laughed; he couldn't help it. What she was saying sounded so ridiculous. "Don't you think you're blowing this all out of proportion?"

Lani jumped to her feet. "I should have known you wouldn't understand."

"No, don't stomp off in a tizzy." Wes grabbed her, his fingers closing around her narrow wrists, and pulled her back down so that she was sitting on the edge of the lounge chair, facing him. "I wasn't making fun of you. I just..." He laughed again, softly.

Lani tugged at her hands.

"No, wait, I'm sorry, Moonmaid. Really." He tightened his grip fractionally, just enough to keep her from pulling loose, and tried to keep his face straight. "But try to see it from my perspective."

"Which is?" she said with all the hauteur of her grandmother at her most autocratic.

"You're telling me that your grandmother, that tiny, gentle, refined woman, is trying to get you married off just to get you to quit running some business she doesn't approve of?" Absently, as if he were unaware of it, both thumbs began caressing the fragile bones in the backs of her wrists. "And that she'd picked me as some sort of sacrificial goat?"

"Yes." Almost against her will, Lani's hands relaxed in his. "That's exactly what I'm telling you."

"Do you realize how medieval that sounds?"

"Yes."

"And completely ridiculous?"

Lani nodded, her eyes on his caressing thumbs. The heat he was generating was slowly working its way up her arms, melting her bones as it went. "Yes."

"Well, there you are."

She lifted her eyes to his; soft, black fathomless eyes that seemed to gather all the mysterious light of the moon in their centers. "There I am—where?" she murmured.

Wes felt his stomach tighten. Fire licked at his groin. "There you are, ah," his caressing hands stilled, tightened, pulling her a tiny bit closer so that their knees were almost touching. Hers were rounded and bare and sweetly dimpled, his were denim-clad and motionless with the effort to keep them from opening wide and pulling her between them. "What I mean is, you don't have to go along with your grandmother's plan. Not if you don't want to."

"I don't," she said softly, trying to believe it.

"And I don't have to go along with it, either," he said, just as softly. They were almost whispering. "So, it's simple. We won't."

"We won't?" She wondered if she sounded as disappointed as she felt.

Wes nodded, wondering if he really meant anything of what he'd just said. Of what he was still saying. "That's right. We won't." His smile was gently teasing, his voice a soft caress. "And she can't make us."

"So there!" Lani added, like a little girl sassing her mother behind her back.

Wes laughed. "So there," he agreed, and pulled her closer. Their knees touched. Their eyes met. They stared at each other for a long, heated moment. Questions but no answers. Need but no commitment. Desire but no love.

Lani was the first to look away. She edged back on the lounge and pulled her hands from his. It was like pushing away from the table when she was still hungry. "Well, now that that's settled," she said shakily, looking anywhere but at the man sitting across from her with his blue eyes as hot as flame and his hands closed into fists on his knees. "I guess I'd better go back—" helplessly, her eyes flickered to his, then away "—to bed," she said, low, and stood up in a rush.

"Yes, I guess you'd better," Wes agreed.

But Lani didn't move. She knew she should, but she couldn't. Something—the way he sat there, the heat sizzling between them, the nagging feeling that something more needed to be said—kept her rooted to the spot. She knew that there could be nothing real or lasting in a feeling less than twelve hours old, no matter how intense. And she didn't want to be there anyway, not really, because she didn't have time for it, wasn't ready for it. And yet, knowing all that, she still didn't move. The night sky lightened almost imperceptibly as she stood there, the darkness turning pink at the edges with the coming of the morning sun. "Wes, I . . ."

He looked up. "If you're going, you'd better go now," he said, low. "While you still can."

"I . . ." Lani began again, wanting to say something but not sure what.

"Too late." He surged to his feet in one quick movement and took her in his arms. Before she could say a word, make a protest, murmur an assent, his mouth came down on hers.

It was as hot as his eyes had been. Hot and skillful, tender and demanding. His tongue snaked out, silently imploring her to part her lips for him.

Passion surged through Lani, urging her to surrender. Alarm came skittering close behind, screaming at her to resist. She wanted to pull him closer and push him away. She wanted to stay in his arms forever, and she wanted to run to the safety of her room and never come out. She wanted him desperately and she wanted, just as desperately, not to want him. Her hands fluttered up and pushed at his shoulders, but softly. So softly. But he felt it and raised his head.

Their eyes met; wide black eyes staring into intense, flaming blue, both full of yearning, rife with the intense longing they had roused in each other.

There should be some anger, she thought vaguely, trying very hard to summon up some emotion other than the longing that was raging through her. Some outrage that he had kissed her against her will and turned her life upside-down in the process. But there was nothing except need.

"Let me go," she said, closing her eyes against the answering need in his. She didn't want him to want her! She didn't want to want him! It didn't fit in with her plans. Or her life.

She heard him breathe deeply, raggedly. "I'm sorry, Moonmaid," he said, his hands sliding from her shoulders as he let her go.

"So am I," she whispered, and then she turned and ran across the lawn to her room.

5

SHE WAS TREMBLING when she reached her room. Trembling and aroused and afraid. Of what, she wasn't quite sure. That he would follow her? That she would turn and beckon him to come to her? She didn't know. To forestall either occurrence, she pushed the glass doors shut, drawing first the gauzy white undercurtains over them and then the heavier flowered drapes. Then she felt like a fool for having barricaded herself in like some captured Puritan maiden fleeing the lecherous advances of a bare-chested pirate.

"Damn!" She kicked at her pillow, sending it sailing across the room to land with a dull thud against the opposite wall. She dropped to the stool in front of her dressing table and turned on the lamp, confronting the woman in the mirror.

Captured maiden, indeed, she scoffed at herself, scowling at her reflection. But the face that looked back at her wasn't as far removed from that fanciful image as she would have liked to believe. Her cheeks were flushed, her eyes filled with conflicting emotions, her lips parted and moist, her hair tousled from sleep.

She lifted a hand, smoothing the bangs back from her forehead. She hadn't bothered to run a comb through it when she went foraging for her snack because she hadn't expected anyone else to be up. "Surprise, surprise," she whispered, reaching for her hairbrush. With slow absent strokes, she began to untangle her hair.

If only she could untangle the emotions in her eyes so easily! They gazed back at her, huge and vaguely unfocused. Still full of want and wonder. Still full of *him*. She stared intently into her own eyes. Is that what he'd seen when he'd stood there on the lanai and looked down at her? This intense, aching want that she couldn't remember ever having experienced before? This heat? The hand holding the brush dropped to her lap.

Oh, God, what was the matter with her?

But she knew. And, typically, she forced herself to face it head-on, without embellishments or evasions.

It was physical desire, pure and simple. Or, maybe, she thought, smiling wryly at her reflection, not so pure. But certainly simple. As basic as man and woman. As elemental as Adam and Eve. As fundamental as a kiss. Only, she thought wistfully, her thumb rubbing over the bristles of the brush, if she had to develop an instant case of lust for someone, why did it have to happen now?

In a year, maybe two, when she had Sail Away running smoothly, she might be ready for a serious relationship. But not now. She didn't have time for it now. And especially not with some hot-shot lawyer from the mainland, a man handpicked by her grandmother for the role. Even if he did have the broadest shoulders and the bluest eyes she'd ever seen. Not to mention a love for sailing that seemed to match her own and a sense of humor that . . .

Lani tossed the brush on her dressing table with a small snort of disgust. Hadn't she just decided that it was purely physical? That she had no time for romance? Yet here she sat, like some dippy airhead, thinking up reasons to get involved with him, rationalizing it into more than it really was.

"What you feel is physical attraction, nothing more," she told the woman in the mirror. "You let yourself get carried

away by a pair of broad shoulders and a wicked grin and
the power of suggestion, and you think it's—" she couldn't
quite meet her own eyes in the mirror "—something else.
Well, it isn't! So forget it. Just stop thinking about him altogether."

With that bit of good advice to herself, she rose from the
dressing table and headed for the shower, determined to get
on with things as if nothing had happened. If she hurried,
she could be gone before the rest of the household stirred.
It seemed like a good plan. She needed to be at the Sail Away
office early, anyway. She had two short tours booked for
today and an overnight to Maui. Rich was expected back
this morning with the schooner, *Destiner*. He'd been captaining a two-week cruise around the islands and, since the
tourist family included three teenage boys, she knew there'd
be plenty of cleanup and brass polishing before *Destiner* was
shipshape again.

The Sail Away office could use a good cleaning, too, she
thought, vigorously shampooing her hair under the pierc-
ing spray of the shower. Usually she tidied up as needed, but
lately there had been so many short-day and weekend
bookings, as well as the longer cruises that Rich had been
called on to captain, that there had been little time for any
but absolutely necessary housekeeping. She'd have to see
about getting one of the high school kids that crewed for Sail
Away to do a few chores. Almost any one of them would
be glad of the extra dollars.

Stepping from the shower, she wrapped a towel around
her dripping hair and used another to pat herself dry before
applying a body moisturizer and sunscreen, and shrugging
into a short white terry robe. As she used a blow-dryer and
brush on her hair, taming it into shining sleekness, she
mentally went over the rest of her schedule for the day, using all her considerable willpower to keep out any stray

thought of Wes Adams and the kiss they had shared on the lanai.

She had an appointment to see a man from a local travel agency about Sail Away's tours. He wanted her to consider booking through his agency. Lani didn't think she would; her father had always done his own bookings and made his own schedules. Kept you more independent and flexible, he'd said, and allowed you to pick and choose your own customers. Lani agreed with those sentiments but she'd been having some trouble with the bookings lately and the guy from the travel agency had been so insistent that she'd found herself agreeing to listen to his pitch.

Rich should be back by midmorning with his tour and Lani made it a point to be on hand to greet her hopefully satisfied customers and find out if all had gone well. Then there were the two cruises she had scheduled for herself today—one for three teachers from the mainland who wanted to "Go out for an hour or so," they'd said, "and take pictures of the island," the other was a family on vacation who wanted basically the same thing. Then there was an overnight for a pair of honeymooners who wanted a romantic midnight sail to Maui, where they would spend the night, before she'd bring them back in the morning.

And, as always, as sure as death and taxes, was the dratted paperwork. Bills and ledgers and who knew what else to be fit in whenever she found the time to tend to them. And she had to admit, grimacing as she pulled a pair of wildly flowered shorts up over her hips, that since she hated the paperwork, she usually found very little time to do it. This, however, had to change. And soon. She couldn't afford to give short shrift to the paperwork any longer. She'd drown in it before long if she went on the way she did—and Sail Away would go down with her.

She would dig into it first thing this morning, she promised herself, knotting the tails of a bright blue shirt at her
waist. She'd make some progress in that pile of papers in her
In basket before anything else had a chance to interfere if it
killed her. And it very well might, she thought, catching up
her canvas tote bag as she pushed open the door to her room
and, barefoot, stepped outside.

It was another balmy, sunshiny day and, as a native of
the islands, Lani hardly noticed it. What she did notice,
though, was the glass-topped table already set for three and
the two people eating and chatting with each other over the
low centerpiece of lacy greens and miniature orchids.

Should have gone out through the hallway, she thought,
feeling her blood begin to heat at the mere sight of Sumiko's breakfast companion. She half turned to do just that,
hoping to make an unseen getaway, when Sumiko noticed
her, hovering there on the lanai in front of her bedroom, and
lifted her hand, motioning her granddaughter to join them.

Too late now, Lani told herself. Taking a deep breath, she
forcibly banished all memories of the morning's encounter
from her mind. Fixing a bright smile on her face, she strode
briskly across the garden to where Wes and her grandmother were having breakfast.

"Good morning, Gran," she said, bending to give Sumiko a light kiss on the cheek as she spoke. "'Morning,
Wes," she added casually, without looking directly at him.
It was better, she decided, if she didn't look at him. She
turned to accept a steaming cup of tea from Fomi. "Um-mm,
this hits the spot, Fomi. *Mahalo,*" she said, thanking her.
"But no breakfast for me this morning. No time."

"Please sit down, Granddaughter," said Sumiko, "and let
our guest finish his coffee before you go rushing off. I am
sure ten minutes will not affect you critically."

Lani continued to stand, sipping her tea. "Can't, Gran," she said, trying to appear hurried and coolly unruffled at the same time. Trying, too, to pretend that she didn't feel Wes's eyes caressing every inch of her bare legs beneath her shorts. "I've got a million things waiting at the office today, and I expect Rich back this morning, too."

"And where has Richard been that you must expect him back?"

"He had a two-week cruise," Lani said, making an effort to stifle her impatience. Complete forgetfulness on any aspect of Sail Away was part of her grandmother's game plan. Sumiko simply acted as if it didn't exist. And Lani acted as if it didn't bother her. "I'm sure I must have mentioned it."

"I do not think so," Sumiko said serenely.

Lani put her cup down with exaggerated care, resisting the urge to bang it on the table. "I really have to get going," she said firmly, unable to act quite so unconcerned as usual this morning.

Wes rose at her words, forestalling any reply from Sumiko. "I've finished my coffee, Mrs. Walsh-san. No, don't get up." His large hand on her shoulder held her gently in her seat. "Have another cup of tea and enjoy this beautiful morning. I'll just get my briefcase," he said, looking at Lani, "and we can be off." Without waiting for an answer, he turned and walked around the lanai to his room.

"Does he think he's going with me?" asked Lani, her eyes on his retreating back. He looked sleek and formidable and as sexy as all hell in a lightweight tan suit.

Sumiko nodded, idly stirring her tea. "Regrettably, the Mercedes required a more lengthy repair than Hiroshi anticipated and it is not available for Wesley's use just yet. I naturally assumed that you would be willing to do our guest this small service and drive him to David's office." She looked up at her granddaughter innocently. "Of course, if this inconveniences you greatly, we can make other arrangements. I could ask David to come and pick Wesley up," she suggested. "Or, perhaps—" she frowned slightly "—a taxi, if David is too busy."

Lani ignored the last part of her grandmother's statement, knowing it had only been said for effect. There was no way Wes was going anywhere in a taxi if Sumiko had anything to say about it. "Do I pick him up tonight, too?" Lani asked, a touch of rebellion in her tone.

"No, my dear. I would not impose upon you to such an extent," Sumiko answered.

Lani listened for the sarcasm under her grandmother's words but didn't hear any. She never did. Sumiko could make the most outrageous, infuriating, even insulting statements without ever changing her sweet, melodious tone of voice. It was, as Lani's father had said on more than one occasion, a damned sight more unnerving that way. Lani wholeheartedly agreed with him.

"The car should be delivered to David's office this afternoon, so neither you nor Wesley will be inconvenienced any more than necessary," Sumiko added serenely, seemingly unaware of the slight moue of dissatisfaction pursing her granddaughter's lips. "Does that meet with your approval, Granddaughter?"

"Yes, of course. Sounds wonderful," she said dryly.

Sumiko's eyes clouded slightly at her granddaughter's tone, her expression bordering on bewildered hurt.

Lani bent and pressed her soft cheek to her grandmother's. "I'm sorry, Gran," she said, instantly contrite, even though she knew the expression was more than half-manufactured. "I didn't mean to sound like a brat." Catching sight of Wes, briefcase in hand, she added in a whisper, "I'll deliver him safely to Dave and I'll be as gracious about it as you would be, okay?" she said, planting another soft kiss on Sumiko's even softer cheek.

Then, not waiting for an answer, she straightened gracefully and moved toward the foyer, entering just ahead of Wes. Pausing there, she slipped quickly into her Topsiders and hurried outside to start the Jeep, leaving Wes to put his own shoes on. Or Sumiko could do it for him. Lani chuckled outright at the picture that thought conjured up. She couldn't remember her grandmother kneeling to help anyone with their shoes since her grandfather's death. And she wasn't likely to do it now. Still, the thought was diverting.

When Wes reached the Jeep he leaned into it, one hand braced on the fringed top overhead, one hand reaching to brush off the sandy seat. His dark blue knit tie swung forward, away from the awesome dimensions of a chest covered by the baby-blue pinstripes of his crisp, cotton shirt. Lani pushed in the clutch and pretended not to notice.

"Giving me the silent treatment?" he inquired affably as he slid in beside her.

Lani let the clutch out and eased the Jeep into first. As always, the gears ground together. She darted a quick glance at him to see if he'd noticed.

He smiled at her.

Lani ignored him, ostensibly concentrating on maneuvering the Jeep out of the circular driveway and onto Maunalani Drive.

"Would it help if I apologize?" asked the man beside her.

"I'm surprised you feel you have anything to apologize for," she said, still not looking at him.

"I don't," he answered. "But it's obvious that you think I do, so—" She sensed rather than saw his shrug. "If it'll make you feel better, I'm sor—"

"I don't," she said quickly, interrupting him.

"You don't what?"

"I don't feel you have anything to apologize for."

He shifted in his seat to face her, one arm coming up to rest on the back of the seat. "Oh?"

"No." She darted another quick glance at him. He was staring at her, his expression curiously still and expectant. His fingers were mere inches from her shoulder. She could feel the heat radiating from them, arcing across those scant few inches like charges of electricity. "You didn't do anything except kiss me," she said, shrugging as if it were no big deal. "Nothing to apologize for in that."

"Then why did you take off like a scared rabbit?"

She shrugged again, then shook her head, unable to think of a reason. At least, not a reason she could tell him. She had no intention of blurting out the fact that his kiss had shaken her right down to her toes.

"Well?" he prodded, unable to let it go. The tip of his index finger stretched out, just touching the fabric of her shirt.

She shot him another quick look out of the corner of her eye. Those intensely blue, implacable lawyer's eyes looked back at her. His finger moved, just barely, back and forth against her shirt sleeve. "I don't want to get involved," she said, feeling the light caress as acutely as if he were touching her skin. "I haven't got time for a relationship at this stage of my life."

His finger stilled. Retreated. "No," he agreed, shifting to face forward in his seat again. "Neither do I."

At least, that's what he'd been telling himself ever since he'd given in to the urge to take her in his arms and kiss her. When he flew over here, his plan had been to clear up this problem at Walsh Imports and then buy himself a good, seaworthy boat and take off on a long solitary ocean voyage. That was still his plan. No way did a "relationship" fit into that plan.

But what the hell, he thought, trying to put it in perspective, *one kiss does not a relationship make.* Not even a kiss that had knocked him right on his can.

"Are you planning on doing any sightseeing while you're here?" Lani asked suddenly, unable to bear his silence any longer. Her tone, deliberately friendly but impersonal, was the same one she used to make small talk with Sail Away customers.

Wes gave her a long, considering look. "So we're just going to pretend it never happened?" he said.

Lani gave a small, quick nod. "Yes. I think it's best that way." It was the only way. "Don't you?"

His hesitation was brief. "Yes," he agreed tightly, wondering if he really did. But, hell, it was best. "So," he said, slumping down in the seat a little. "What do you suggest?"

"Suggest?"

"Sightseeing."

"Oh. Well, if you've never spent any time here before there's Pearl Harbor for starters," she began, forcing herself to sound bright and interested and not as if his quick agreement had left her feeling bereft. "Not the regular tourist charters, though. The military one is better, much more informative. And then there's the National Cemetery of the Pacific at Punchbowl Crater. It's a very sobering sight, those almost endless rows of white markers. In Hawaiian it's called *Puowiana* and means the Hill of Sacrifice. Most malihini want to see the Blow Hole at Koko Head," she continued in her best tour guide voice, "and the Kodak Hula Show in Kapiolani Park. It's a little corny but the hula is authentic and well done. And it's free." She considered briefly, her head tilted in thought, her forehead wrinkled beneath the red baseball cap. Strands of glossy hair blew around her face. "There's the Polynesian Cultural Center. That's very nice. And Waikiki Beach and Sea Life Park.

Though I don't guess you'd go in for trained seals and porpoises, would you?"

He ignored her question and asked one of his own. "Malihini?"

"That's you," she answered. "Malihini is Hawaiian for newcomer or stranger. After you've been here awhile and know *mauka* from *makai*, you'll be a *kama'aina*, an old-timer."

"*Mauka* and *makai* being?" he asked, doing his part to keep the conversation on an impersonal level when what he really wanted to do was force her to pull this ramshackle Jeep over to the side of the road so that he could shut her luscious little mouth with his own.

"That's the Hawaiian way of giving directions," Lani told him, feeling safer now on familiar, impersonal ground. If they could just keep it up, she thought, she'd be able to forget about that kiss. Maybe. In a pig's eye. "*Mauka* means toward the mountains and *makai* means toward the sea. So, if you were standing on Waikiki Beach, for instance, and wanted to get back to the house you'd go about two miles toward Diamond Head and then *mauka* until you got there. See?"

"I see," he said dryly. "You're very informative."

"I have to know a lot about the islands. Tourists always want to know a few native words and a little history. And the women always want to know the best places to shop," she added, turning into the mammoth underground parking lot of the Ala Moana Shopping Center. Now she was safe, she thought, maneuvering the Jeep into a space in the nearly empty lot. She swung her legs over the side of the Jeep and stood up, automatically tossing her baseball cap and sunglasses onto the seat. "It's been ages since I've been here early enough to see it this empty," she remarked, shouldering her tote bag. "Usually finding a parking space takes all morning."

They walked through the maze of shops and eateries, Lani a step or two in the lead, passing only store employees on their way to work at this early hour. Walsh Imports was located on the second level of the mall. The two narrow front windows were already undraped, the day's display visible behind the sparkling glass. Lani scarcely had time to admire the elegant simplicity of the display before the front door opened inward.

"Ah, Ms MacPherson-san." David Yamazaki greeted his employer's granddaughter with a slight bow, always formally correct despite the fact that he'd known her since she was a child. "And Mr. Adams-san." His greeting to Wes was more on the level of equals, one businessman to another. "I bid you aloha," he said with a smile, extending his hand as he bowed.

"Thank you." Wes smiled and shook the offered hand.

Lani stood a little back while the men exchanged greetings, feeling a bit out of place in her loud flowered shorts and casually knotted shirt amid all the beautiful and valuable antiques and the men in their impeccably tailored suits. She told herself that that was the only reason she was eager to be on her way. That and the pile of work waiting on her desk. It had nothing to do with the way Wes made her feel.

"Well," she said when they paused in their exchange of pleasantries. "I guess I'll be going now. Got a busy day ahead of me." She smiled pleasantly to both men. "Gran said that her car would be delivered to you this afternoon, Wes, so I'll see you tomorrow sometime, okay?"

"I won't see you at dinner tonight?"

She shook her head, automatically reaching up to brush back the hair that caressed her cheek. "I've got an all-night cruise to Maui. I won't be home until sometime tomorrow."

"Is your grandmother aware of your plans?" Dave Yamazaki inquired with a slight frown.

"I'll call her from the Sail Away office," Lani assured him, trying not to show her irritation at yet another person's interference, however subtle, in the way she ran her business.

"Coward," Wes said softly.

Lani ignored him. "You two have a good day," she said, moving toward the front door.

"You will be careful, Ms MacPherson-san?" Dave said as he opened it for her. "The Molokai Channel can be tricky. But you would know that, of course," he acknowledged quickly, seeing her frown.

"Yes, I'll be careful. I promise." She patted the hand at her elbow. "Thank you for caring." Her eyes lifted to Wes's for a fleeting second. "Aloha, Wes."

"Take care, Moonmaid," he said as she turned away.

SANDWICHED BETWEEN a travel agency and a fast-food seafood restaurant, the Sail Away office faced Ala Wai Harbor. The view from its plate-glass window encompassed the busy harbor, the yacht club building and the endless expanse of clear blue ocean visible from the west end of Waikiki Beach. It was easily accessible to the tourists who wandered over from nearby hotels and surrounding shops. There was an awning over the front door of the same blue and yellow striped fabric as the Jeep top and the words Thomas MacPherson, Owner still appeared under the company name. Lani hadn't yet had the heart to have it changed. She pushed open the door and switched on the lights, looking with dismay at the untidy room.

Under the clutter it was an attractive office. The walls were painted a pale blue and held a collection of sailing pictures and posters. Thomas MacPherson smiled down at his daughter from several photos, as did Lani herself, and Rich, and any number of the mostly high school age employees who at one time or another had crewed for Sail Away. There were pictures of happy Sail Away customers, too—standing at the helm of a sailboat or posing proudly beside a prize marlin or a record-weight yellow fin tuna. A ship's clock, mounted in a ship's wheel, hung behind the desk. Five faded, navy canvas directors chairs and a single filing cabinet completed the office's furnishings.

The desk was all but hidden beneath stacks of travel brochures, piloting charts, island maps and sailing magazines. The wastebasket was full to overflowing, the visitor's chairs each held a jumble of bright orange life vests and yellow foul-weather gear. The single plant atop the file cabinet looked as if it had already died of thirst.

The door to the small storage room stood open, and through it Lani could see Rich's diving gear and her own seldom-used surfboard, along with a motley assortment of swim fins, air mats and damp beach towels. The top of a bikini, hers presumably, hung on the doorknob.

Lani groaned, wondering if Kim, her office helper, had come in at all yesterday. It certainly didn't look as if she had. But then, Lani wondered, had she ever actually *told* the teenager that housekeeping was part of her job? Probably not, she decided. And if she hadn't told her, then Kim wouldn't see any reason to do it.

"I'm sorry, Pop," she said, as if he were in the room. Like the old salt he was, her father had always kept the office as shipshape as the cabin of a sailboat—a place for everything and everything in its place. And she agreed with him.

Resolutely she began attacking the worst of it. She gathered up the life vests and foul-weather gear first, hanging them to dry on their hooks in the storage room, and then emptied the wastebasket into one of the large containers in the alley behind the office. She rescued the bikini top from the doorknob, idly wondering where the bottoms were, and stuffed it, and the towels, into a canvas laundry sack to be taken home and washed. Lastly, she dealt with the mess on her desk by dividing the material between the wire In and Out baskets set on either side, promising herself that she would go through it later to decide where it really belonged. Kim, she was happy to note, had shown up yesterday; the teen movie magazines left on the desk were proof of that.

She was trying to decide whether to begin straightening out the tangle of diving and swim gear in the storage room or start digging into the paperwork when the ship's clock chimed three bells. Nine-thirty, she translated without conscious thought. The man from the travel agency would arrive any minute.

She hurried out of the storage room, pulling the door closed behind her and yanked open the lower drawer of her desk. It held a neat stack of blue and yellow T-shirts like the one she had worn yesterday emblazoned with the company logo. Grabbing the top one, she quickly changed tops, exchanging her bright blue shirt for a softer blue T-shirt. She had just turned the Closed sign to Open and was raising the bamboo shade on the plate-glass window when the front door opened.

"Good morning," she said brightly, winding the drawstring around its hook before turning around. Her visitor was wearing tailored white pants, a loud Hawaiian shirt in shades of yellow and orange, and white deck shoes. Too many gold chains tangled with the polished ebony of a tra-

ditional *kukui* nut necklace. His round, bald head was
deeply tanned, fringed by an inch wide strip of graying hair.
"Mr. Larson?"

"Yes, I'm Larson. Carl Larson."

"Won't you sit down, please?" invited Lani. "I'm afraid I
can't offer you coffee. We seem to be out. But I do have some
cold Cokes or—"

"Nothing thanks, honey," he interrupted. He looked
pointedly at the clock above the desk. "Will Mr. Mac-
Pherson be delayed long?"

"I'm Ms MacPherson." Lani put a subtle emphasis on the
Ms and deliberately moved behind her desk to sit in the
canvas chair labeled Captain. "There is no Mr. Mac-
Pherson."

"It says Thomas MacPherson on the window," he pointed
out.

"He was my father." Lani paused a minute to let that sink
in. "What can I do for you?"

"I spoke to a Richard Billings a few weeks ago," he said.
"Is he around?"

When would he have talked to Rich? And why? "No, he's
captaining a cruise."

"When will he be back?"

"This morning, as it happens. But he can't help you," she
said firmly. "I'm not the secretary here, Mr. Larson. I'm the
owner of Sail Away Tours. Rich Billings works for me."
Maybe that would get through to him.

"And there's no man I could talk to?"

Lani stifled a sigh; she'd thought men like him were a
dying breed. "I'm afraid not," she said, trying for humor. It
was easier than getting angry. "So it looks like you're stuck
with me." *But not for long*, she promised herself. She'd listen to his pitch because there was no polite way out of it

now, but she wasn't buying. Not from a dyed-in-the-wool male chauvinist oinker. "Shall we get down to business?"

He wavered for a second, looking as if he might leave rather than do business with a mere woman. *Good*, Lani thought, silently urging him out, *go*. But he shrugged and sat down, opening a folder on her desk. He had just gotten as far as explaining the Larson Holiday Travel philosophy when the telephone rang.

With a soft "Excuse me" Lani picked it up. "Sail Away Tours. How can I help you?"

"Lani? Al Duffy," the voice on the other end stated unnecessarily.

"Hi, Al," she answered with forced brightness, recognizing that the tone of his voice meant trouble. Al Duffy had never been one of her favorite people. His attitudes toward women were too much like the man sitting across from her. But he'd been with Sail Away for years, running the fishing end of the business in a competent, if not exactly gracious, manner. "What's up?" she asked, dreading the answer.

"Don't 'Hi, Al,' me," he growled. "Who the hell booked two parties on the *Pride* for today? I got a bunch of haoles here," he said, using the Hawaiian word for Caucasian, "all decked out and ready to go and—"

"Calm down, Al," she interrupted smoothly. "I can't hear a word when you're hollering like that."

"I said, I got a bunch of haoles here, expectin' to go out on the *Pride* this mornin'," he repeated in a slightly lower tone. "I wanna know who did it."

"Aren't any of the other boats available?"

"Nary a one. The *Gluttony* is in dry dock gettin' her bottom scraped and we're still waitin' on that motor part for the *Lust*. But all the other sins are out," he said with satisfaction. "It's been a damned busy season."

"All right, Al, hold on a minute." She caught the receiver between her ear and shoulder and began riffling the desk for her schedule book. "I'll be just a minute," she said to the man across from her. "Al?" She had the book open to the proper page.

"Yeah, I'm here."

"The first booking I have listed is a Mr. Angelo, party of six. He made his reservation months ago. I took the information. The second is a Mr. Evans, party of one, made last week."

"And who's the lame-brained knucklehead who took that reservation?"

"The handwriting isn't mine or Rich's. It must be that new girl we hired to help out around here."

"You let anyone, just anyone, take bookings?" His voice had risen again, clearly audible to both the occupants in the small office.

Lani smiled sheepishly across the desk, silently cursing Al for putting her in this embarrassing position. Carl Larson was sitting in one of her visitor's chairs with a satisfied smirk on his face, clearly feeling that he'd been right in his first assessment of her—and thereby all women's—business ability.

"Al," she said when he paused for breath. "Al. I'm sorry, okay? I really am. I'll make sure this doesn't happen again."

"That doesn't help me now!"

"I know. But can't you take them all?" Why was he being so damned difficult, anyway? One extra passenger wasn't a catastrophe by any means, even if Mr. Angelo had reserved the entire boat. "Just offer Mr. Angelo a discount." That was the usual procedure when a mix-up like this occurred. "Or did you already try—"

"Already done," Al interrupted. "And at full price. They're gettin' loaded now."

"Well, then what's the problem?" she said in exasperation.

"Just wanted to make sure it doesn't happen again."

He hung up, leaving Lani holding a dead receiver. With a slight, puzzled shake of her head she laid it back in its cradle and turned her attention back to her visitor.

"I'm sorry for the interruption." She gestured toward the telephone. "A small scheduling problem. Now, where were we?"

"Well, your little scheduling problem illustrates just how we can help you," Carl Larson said. "Do you have these mix-ups often, honey?"

"Very rarely," she answered coolly, annoyed by his use of the endearment. "We have a new girl working in the office. Apparently she needs a little more instruction on booking procedures," she continued, unconsciously slipping into the formal tones used by her grandmother. "But, as you heard," she said, with a slight lift of her hand toward the phone, "the problem has been satisfactorily resolved."

"But if the two parties had been bigger?" he persisted.

She shrugged. "The party with the earliest reservations would naturally have first priority. But, in any case, Al would have worked it out." *Maybe*, she added silently.

"Al?"

"Yes, Al Duffy. He works for me, too, Mr. Larson. Handles all the fishing excursions from our office in Haliewa. But," she added, lest he should get the idea that Al might be the man he could talk to, "he has no authority beyond that."

"So you really do run this operation all by yourself." He shook his head in disbelief. "Such a pretty little girl, too."

"I assure you, my looks have nothing to do with it," she said dryly. "Now, shall we get back to business?" She reached out and picked up several of the glossy travel pamphlets from the folder he had opened on her desk. She fanned them in her hands like a deck of cards, looking thoughtfully at the activities and tours offered. "If we were to reach an agreement," she said, "then your travel agency would make up brochures like these on Sail Away?"

"We would."

"And you'd handle all the bookings?"

"That's the whole idea, honey."

Lani made a neat stack of the pamphlets and laid them back in the folder. This slick, packaged approach was all wrong for Sail Away. "I'm sorry, Mr. Larson, I seem to have wasted your time. You see, Sail Away offers a very personal service and this—" she said, waving her hand over the glossy brochures "—would make it less so. We don't offer one particular package. Each of our adventures is just that. An adventure. Tailored to the customer's specific wants and priced accordingly." She shook her head. "There's no way I could give you an 'average' tour or quote any fixed price to print in a pamphlet."

"That's hardly standard business practice." His expression clearly said that he expected no better from a woman.

"Perhaps," agreed Lani. "But then, Sail Away isn't a standard business. Oh, the Seven Sins could be neatly categorized. Fishing trips hardly vary. But our sailing tours are never the same. Some customers want a full crew, some want to do the actual sailing themselves and require only a captain. We have people who want to anchor at dock every night and eat in a fancy restaurant. Others ask that we supply a cook and full provisions." She stood up. "I'm sorry for wasting your time." She extended her hand. After a brief pause, he took it. "I do hope you understand why I feel we can't do business."

His look said plainly that he didn't but, possibly feeling that further discussion would be unproductive, he gathered up his brochures. "Thank you for your time, Ms

MacPherson," he said stiffly, using her name for the first time.

"Thank you, Mr. Larson," she returned, allowing herself a loud sigh of relief when the door closed firmly behind him.

Even if she had been thinking about doing business with his travel agency, meeting him would have changed her mind. He was a real oinker, through and through. Calling her "honey," acting as if she probably couldn't cross the street by herself. It always amazed her when she ran into a man with an attitude like his. Although why it did, she didn't know, since many of the men in her line of business were the same. The older and middle-aged ones, anyway. They were full of macho seafaring tradition and superstition. They believed that women had no place at sea, except as sirens luring sailors to their death, or omens of bad luck if one should actually step foot on a boat.

Even her father—God rest his salty old soul—had had his share of those superstitions. He just hadn't applied any of them to his daughter. He'd sent her to the Marine Academy to get her piloting and navigational certificates and, later, her charter captain's license, right alongside all the old sea dogs who were his friends, not caring a whit that they would prefer she wasn't there.

She leaned back in her chair, balancing it on two legs, wondering if Wes Adams was one of those "old salts" who believed that women belonged on the shore, waving their men goodbye. Somehow she didn't think so. But then, she thought, her mouth curving into a dreamy smile, what could you tell about a man from a few longing looks and one kiss. Even if that one kiss *had* scorched her right down to her smallest toe?

"I wonder if his second one will feel the same," she said to herself, forgetting that she'd decided there would be no second one.

"Whose second what?" said a voice from the door.

6

LANI'S CHAIR SLAMMED FORWARD onto all four legs. "Rich!" she squeaked, grabbing the edge of the desk with both hands to steady herself.

He grinned. "Yeah, it's me," he said, standing in the open doorway with one brown hand resting lightly on the knob. Tanned to a deep mahogany, wearing ragged cutoff jeans and the much larger twin to Lani's T-shirt, his bare feet laced into deck shoes, his shaggy, pale blond hair curling over his ears, Rich Billings was the epitome of the All-American Surfer.

"Whose second what?" he asked again, swinging the door shut with a careless bang. He dropped into the canvas chair recently vacated by Mr. Larson and lifted his sneakered feet to Lani's desk.

"Get your big feet off my desk," she said, ignoring his question.

"My, my, aren't we snappy this morning." His voice was full of the teasing affection of a beloved brother. "Whose second what?" he repeated.

Lani merely glared at him.

"Okay, okay. So you don't want to talk about it. My feet are on the floor," he added placatingly, slouching even further as he stretched his bare, hairy legs out in front of him and crossed his bony ankles. "I didn't mean to get on your bad side right off."

"You're not on my bad side," she relented, smiling. He was as aggravating as the very devil but she loved him.

"Prove it." He lifted his size-twelve feet to the edge of the desk again. "Get me a Coke."

Lani's eyes narrowed warningly but she got up and went back to the store room for his Coke. "Here," she said, thrusting it into his outstretched hand. "And get your big feet off my desk," she added, pushing them off herself.

They struck the floor with a thump. "Ah, *mahalo*, Lani." He rolled the cold can against his forehead before draining it empty. "Really hits the spot. Got anything to eat?"

Without a word, she opened the middle desk door and began rummaging for the candy bar she remembered seeing there just last week.

"Aren't you going to ask me how it went?" he said, watching her with a fond smile.

"How'd it go?" she obliged absently. "Hey!" Her head snapped up, her hands halted their search. "You're back early."

"I'm not early." He gestured at the ship's clock behind her with the empty can. "I'm right on time."

"The Powers!" Lani slammed the drawer shut and sprang to her feet. "Where are they? Did they enjoy themselves?"

"Take it easy, Squirt," Rich sail lazily. "They're still on *Destiner*, gathering their gear together. I told them I'd go and fetch the boss lady."

"Well, come on." Lani picked up the office keys and stuffed them into the pocket of her shorts, already halfway to the door.

But Rich hadn't budged. "I still haven't had anything to eat," he said reasonably.

"Richard," she warned, but she came back to her desk and began haphazardly pulling open drawers, knowing he wasn't going to move until he'd been fed. "You'd think they'd starved you for two weeks," she said irritably.

"Well, they did. Practically. Especially the little one." He ran a hand through his shaggy hair. "You should have seen that kid put away the groceries," he said admiringly. If there was one thing Rich admired, besides a pretty girl, it was a hearty trencherman. "Only eleven. I don't know where he put it all."

"I don't know where you put it all." She tossed the stale candy bar at him, then switched on her answering machine. "Now, come on."

She was out the door before he rose from the chair, impatiently waiting to lock up. She flipped the Closed sign over, set the hands on the Be Back At clock beneath it to eleven and began walking briskly to cover the half block to the boat slip. She could see *Destiner's* tall masts rocking gently at anchor and, as always, was eager to greet her customers and assure herself that all had gone well.

"Slow down, Squirt," Rich said, dropping a long brown arm over her shoulders, forcing her to his more leisurely pace. "This is beautiful Hawaii, remember?" He made a sweeping gesture with his free arm. "Island paradise, Land of Enchantment. Life moves with leisurely grace." He was quoting from a travel magazine.

Lani smiled good-naturedly at his nonsense, allowing him to set the pace. He was right. It was another beautiful Hawaiian day and, so far, she hadn't taken the time to notice it. The air was soft and warm, conducive to ambling along. The sky was blue and cloudless, allowing a huge butterball of a sun to spill its warmth unobstructed. The sidewalk and docks were busy with people, none of whom seemed to be hurrying anywhere as far as she could tell.

Vacationers in shorts and bright Hawaiian shirts were snapping pictures of the palm trees and the gently rocking boats and of their similarly dressed wives and children. Island teenagers, burned to varying shades of brown, carried surfboards balanced precariously atop their heads or held snorkeling masks and swim fins dangling carelessly at their sides. Children of all shapes, sizes and nationalities laughed and squealed as they scampered among the adults. And then there were the honeymooners.

Lani's gaze wandered over the easily recognizable newlywed couples that Hawaii invariably attracted. They strolled along with their arms looped around each other or their fingers tightly intertwined. Not so much enjoying the sights of Hawaii as enjoying each other.

It was the sight of these honeymooners that brought Lani out of her brief mellow mood, putting her mind, once again, on business. After she'd greeted the Powers and tidied up *Destiner*, she ticked off mentally; she had those two short tours to take care of. Then she'd have to make sure that the *Wave Dancer* was shipshape for the honeymooners' overnight sail to Maui. Unconsciously she quickened her step.

Rich, sensing the change, lengthened his stride to keep up with her. The slight squaring of her shoulders under his arm was enough to tell him that she was once more Ms Lani MacPherson, owner of Sail Away and not just plain Lani, pretty girl enjoying the day.

"Did your grandmother's lawyer show up?" he asked, staring down at the soft curve of her cheek.

Lani stiffened slightly and eased out from under his arm. "Not exactly."

"How can someone not exactly show up?"

She shrugged. "Gerard Adams didn't come himself. He sent his nephew."

"This nephew, he's a lawyer, too?"

"Mm-hm," she said, as if it didn't matter much. But she was very sure that Rich, who knew Sumiko almost as well as she did, would know that it did matter. "Junior partner of the firm, I think."

"How junior a partner?"

"How junior? Oh, I don't know," she said evasively. "Next in line, I guess."

"That makes this—what's his name?"

"Wes Adams," she supplied. Damn! She didn't want to talk about Wes Adams.

"That makes this Wes Adams the heir apparent, then?"

"I guess so," she said irritably. "Why? What difference does it make?"

Rich shrugged. "I don't know. Unless—" He stopped dead in his tracks and looked down at her. "Is he the one whose 'second one' you were wondering about?"

Lani felt herself flushing. "No," she said, and walked faster.

"You're being awfully damned evasive," Rich persisted, staring at her back as she moved away from him.

"And you're being awfully damned nosy," she snapped.

"Well, hey." He caught up with her. "Can you blame me? Before I left on this cruise you were bending my ear with all that stuff about how you were going to send the old guy packing. Only he turns out not to be the old guy after all, and you get as puffed up as a blowfish when I ask about him. What'd he do? Make a pass at you or something?"

"Don't be ridiculous," she said, and ran lightly down the narrow wooden ramp to the slip where *Destiner* was tied to greet the Powers.

She was good with the customers, better even than her father had been, and Rich was content to hang back, giving her time to shake hands all around and ask if they'd enjoyed their trip. Apparently they had because she turned toward him as he ambled down the ramp in her wake.

"Rich," she said enthusiastically, pulling her keys from the pocket of her shorts. "I'm going to run and get the Jeep so we can get everyone back to their hotel." She hugged him lightly in passing. "You did a super job," she whispered. "They're going to recommend us to all their friends."

AN HOUR AND A HALF LATER, the Powers had been safely deposited back at their hotel, *Destiner* had been scrubbed and polished and disinfected, and Rich had gone off to renew his acquaintance with whatever wahine he was currently dating. All without his having learned one real, solid thing about why she didn't want to talk about Wes Adams. Not that he hadn't asked. And prodded. And pushed.

Rich was as nosy as an old woman with nothing to occupy her mind but gossip, and he had appointed himself her keeper long before her father had died. Like any brother, he thought he was entitled to know everything Lani did and said and felt—especially where men were concerned.

"Aw, come on, Squirt," he'd said when they were polishing the brass fixtures on *Destiner*. "You can tell me what this Adams guy has done to bug you. Haven't we always told each other every little thing about our love lives?"

"You may have bragged about yours," she'd retorted in the lofty tones of her grandmother. "I, however, have always been more discreet."

"Only because you've never had much of a love life to brag about," he'd shot back, and she'd laughed and thrown her polishing rag at him.

He left soon after that, helping himself to the company Jeep, and Lani returned to the Sail Away office to get ready for her first cruise of the day. A pleasant, uneventful two hours later she deposited her three satisfied passengers on the dock and began readying the small boat for her next customers.

The afternoon sail went almost as smoothly. The youngest child had thrown up, not from seasickness, her mother assured Lani, but because her father had allowed her to stuff herself full of fast food and ice cream. Unfortunately the child hadn't made it to the edge of the boat in time. Still, she was fine after emptying her stomach and there were no other incidents to mar the afternoon. Lani was left with a pleasant thank-you, a large tip and a guilty smile from the head of the family, and an unpleasant mess to clean off the *Sunbird*'s deck. Then she headed back to the Sail Away office again, intending to grab a clean T-shirt and a quick shower at the harbor's facilities before readying the *Wave Dancer* for tonight's sail.

Kim, her teenage office helper, was waiting with a message when Lani pushed the door open. "Bobby can't make it tonight," she said by way of greeting. "He's been grounded."

"Grounded?" Lani repeated. Bobby was one of the kids that she hired to crew for her occasionally. He was a good sailor but inclined to be a bit wild. "What did he do this time?"

"He took his father's car without permission again," Kim explained, obviously relishing every word. "He's grounded for the rest of the month."

"Great." Lani dropped into one of the canvas chairs in front of the desk and ran a hand through her hair. "Who's available?" she said to Kim.

"Well." Kim squirmed in her chair. "I couldn't get anybody, Lani. I called all the alternates on the list but nobody wants to crew. There's a big beach party tonight and everybody's going."

"You, too?" Lani said, giving the girl a speculative look. Kim had never crewed for her, and Lani had no idea if she knew anything about sailing. But she didn't really need a sailor; Lani could handle *Wave Dancer* by herself. What she needed was someone to see to the wants of her passengers—a waiter, really, to serve the champagne and the picnic that was included in the cost of the cruise.

"Well, I guess, if you really want me to," Kim said, clearly not wanting to make the offer but not knowing how to refuse outright, either. Her voice faded away hopefully.

"No, never mind," Lani said, letting her off the hook. "You'd miss that beach party." And she'd probably get seasick and be no help, anyway. "Damn," Lani said softly, scowling down at her lap.

"I'm sorry, Lani."

Lani looked up. "It's not your fault, Kim," she assured the guilty-looking girl. "If no one can make it, well—" Her shoulders lifted in a shrug, her palms turned up. "What are ya gonna do?"

"I'd be glad to crew for you," said a voice from behind her.

7

LANI SHOT UP out of her chair, turning around in the same motion, needing to confirm with her eyes what she couldn't believe her ears had heard. But her ears had not deceived her. It was Wes.

He stood with one broad shoulder propped against the doorjamb, his left hand thrust into his pants pocket, his tan suit jacket hanging casually over the opposite shoulder, held there by the crooked index finger of his right hand. The knot of his blue knit tie had been loosened, pulled down a bit to allow the top few buttons of his pale blue and white pin-striped shirt to be undone. His cuffs had been unbuttoned, too, and rolled back, revealing his forearms with their dusting of crisp golden hair.

What was it, Lani wondered vaguely, about a man's hairy forearms with the sleeves rolled back that way, that made even the most sensible woman's knees weak? What was it about a starched dress shirt, just slightly rumpled, that made a woman's fingertips itch to touch the man wearing it? And what was it about *him*, dammit, that set her heart to flapping around in her chest like a sail broken loose and snapping in the wind?

"Wes," she said, trying to sound unaffected by his sudden appearance in her office. "What are you doing here?"

"Offering my services."

"As what?"

His lips quirked up at one corner. "As a member of your crew, of course," he said, something in his sparkling eyes hinting that she had a dirty mind for thinking anything else. "What did you think I meant?"

Lani shrugged. "Nothing."

He shifted his stance, levering himself away from the doorjamb, and sauntered into the office. "So," he said, moving forward until the chair she had been sitting in was the only thing between them. "Are you taking me up on my offer?"

Lani took a quick step back and felt the desk hit her thighs. She leaned against it, as if that's what she'd intended to do, and crossed one bare ankle over the other. Her fingers curled around the desk's edge on either side of her hips as his gaze slid down the length of her legs, then back up again. "No, I'm not," she said bluntly, before she could give in to the urge to say yes.

"But, Lani," Kim's voice came from behind her, "you need someone to crew for you."

"Yeah, you need someone to crew for you," Wes echoed. His other hand came out of his pocket to rest lightly on his hip, just where a brown leather belt circled his trim waist. His fingers pointed toward the fashionable flat pleats of his tan slacks. "And I seem to be the only one available."

"Well, yes, but—" Lani hesitated, folding her arms over her chest in an unconscious gesture of self-protection "—you're not dressed to go sailing," she pointed out.

"No problem," he assured her. "I can get what I need at one of the hotel shops." A tilt of his head indicated the hotels and stores that were her neighbors. "I could use a new pair of deck shoes, anyway."

"Why would you want to crew for me?"

He dropped his suit coat across the canvas back of the deck chair between them and leaned forward, capturing the tops of the wooden uprights on either side, one in each hand. "I don't especially relish the idea of crewing for you," he lied, wagging the chair a bit from side to side. "I kind of like being captain of my own boat." That much was true. "But I need to go to Maui." He leaned forward a bit more, his hands braced on the wooden knobs, his long fingers curved around them. "Is that okay with you, Moonmaid?" *Say yes*, he thought, surprising himself with the vehemence of his desire to hear her answer in the affirmative.

Lani wanted very much to say yes. Too much. "Why?" she said instead, her black eyes narrowed suspiciously.

"Because I've heard of a boat that might be exactly what I'm looking for. A forty-five-foot ketch anchored in Lahaina. I was going to fly over and back tomorrow, but since you're headed over there tonight I might as well hitch a ride and save myself—and your grandmother," he added craftily, "some time tomorrow."

"Oh." It was a good reason, one she couldn't very well refuse. And she *was* short one crew member. "Well, I guess you could crew for me then," she said reluctantly.

"Does that mean I can go now?" said Kim from behind her.

Lani turned and glanced at the clock over her head. "No, it doesn't mean you can go now," she said, and then smiled slightly to soften her refusal, remembering how it was to be sixteen with a beach party in the offing. "But you don't have to stay until closing, either," she relented, "so don't look so stricken. I want you to stick around until I've had a chance to take a shower and go over to the deli to get a picnic for our honeymooners. You can leave when I get back, okay?"

"Okay," agreed Kim, relief evident on her round face.

"You have shower facilities?" Wes asked.

"Not me." Reluctantly Lani turned around to face him again. He was still leaning on the back of the chair, his arms straight, his hands braced on the rounded knobs. His tie hung away from his chest, dangling over the seat of the chair. "Ala Wai Harbor does," she said, her eyes on his tie. "They're just beyond the harbor office." She waved a hand in the general direction. "I have a key because I dock here."

"Good." He straightened, picking up his jacket and slinging it over one arm in the same motion. "Then I'll just do some shopping at the Hilton, take a quick shower myself and meet you back here." He tried not to sound too triumphant now that he'd gotten what he wanted but it was hard. He was almost jubilant. It should have bothered him that he felt that way because a woman he'd known less than two days had agreed, under pressure, to spend time with him. "Does that sound okay to you, Moonmaid?"

Lani just stood there, staring. He was still touching the chair with one hand, his thumb rubbing absently, back and forth, over the rounded wooden knob.

"Moonmaid?"

She lifted her eyes from his hand. "Oh, yes, fine," she said faintly, wishing he wouldn't do that, wouldn't call her that, wouldn't look at her the way he was looking at her. It reminded her, much too forcefully, of this morning on the lanai. "The extra key to the shower is on a hook in the storage room," she said a bit breathlessly.

Was she crazy to be letting him sail with her to Maui? she wondered. Was she just asking for trouble by saying yes? But was there any way she could have said no? Even if she'd really wanted to?

She gave herself a hard, mental shake. She'd only said yes to having a crew member. That was all. "Kim, get the key for Mr. Adams," she instructed the girl.

"Sure thing." Kim all but flew to do her boss's bidding.

"I'll meet you over at the boat slip," Lani said to Wes then. *"Wave Dancer* is in number forty-seven. But if you're not there when I'm ready to go," she warned, trying very hard to believe that she meant it. "I'll weigh anchor without you."

LANI MANAGED to take a shower, change into a fresh T-shirt and purchase a suitably romantic meal from the deli in record time. She called her grandmother from the Sail Away office, prepared for an argument about her overnight absence but Sumiko wasn't the least bit put out. Or surprised.

"Wesley was good enough to call me this afternoon so that I would not expect the two of you for dinner," she said, leaving her granddaughter with her mouth hanging inelegantly open.

Lani didn't know whether she was more annoyed with Wes for simply assuming that she'd let him hitch a ride with her, or with her grandmother, for being so ridiculously pleased that he was making the overnight trip to Maui with her. It was probably a toss-up, she decided, reaching for the phone to make a routine weather check. They both ticked her off.

The latest reports revealed the possibility of a small storm but it wasn't due until early the next morning, and the *Wave Dancer* would be snugly berthed in Lahaina's harbor well before then. Her passengers had already said that they wanted to spend some time in the quaint old whaling town and, by the time they were ready for the return trip, the weather would have blown over. If it hadn't, well, all it would mean is a little rain and some wind. The newlyweds could go below if they didn't want to get wet.

They were an attractive couple. Lani judged Brad Jensen to be about twenty-two. A thin, sunburned young man who introduced his younger and equally sunburned wife with obvious pride. "Sheri's never been on a sailboat," he said, settling her on a cushion in the cockpit. "But I've had some experience." Judging by how awkward he was on the boat, Lani had her doubts about that.

Wes arrived just as Lani was finishing her little talk on boat safety and advising her passengers of the possibility of some strong winds. "All set?" he said, reaching for the tie lines to cast off.

"All set," Lani answered, staunchly denying the spurt of excitement that had begun bubbling in her veins when she'd caught sight of him jogging down the dock. For a minute there, she'd thought he wasn't going to make it on time. And then she'd have had to make good her threat and leave without him. Against all her better judgment, she was glad he hadn't missed the boat. "Cast off," she said, smiling at him in spite of herself.

He looked so handsome, so exactly right, in his soft white cotton pants and deck shoes, she thought, watching him out of the corner of her eye as, together, they maneuvered the *Wave Dancer* out of the slip and into the channel. He'd borrowed a blue Sail Away T-shirt from the supply she kept in the office. One of her father's old ones, she thought, since neither hers or Rich's would be big enough. He had a white cable knit sweater tied around his broad shoulders by the sleeves and his curling, sun-streaked hair was still damp from his shower.

The wind was brisk as they left the shelter of the harbor, filling the sails instantly, pushing them out, full and firm, like the curve of a pregnant woman's belly. Lani sat at the tiller, guiding the *Wave Dancer* through the buoy markers and into the open sea. It was dark enough now to switch on the running lights, and the cockpit was bathed in the soft red glow of the instrument panel. The rising moon turned the billowing sails to a ghostly white and danced off the phosphorescence in the boat's wake. It was a magical night, Lani thought, a perfect night for a sail.

Brad and Sheri Jensen apparently thought so, too. They sat nestled together in the forward half of the cockpit, his arm around her shoulders, smiling at each other. Wes was at the bow of the boat, near the rail on the starboard side, neatly coiling the lines that had been used to tie the *Wave Dancer* to the dock. Lani watched approvingly as he moved past her to check the stern lines. Her father would have approved, too. He'd liked a man who kept things shipshape without having to be told.

"Would you get the champagne, Wes?" she said, looking up at him when he stepped down into the cockpit. He was a little behind her and she had to tilt her head back to meet his eyes. The position exposed the long, elegant line of her throat and the small, delicate lobes of her ears.

Wes's right eyebrow lifted in silent query, his eyes devouring her.

"The champagne," she repeated a bit breathlessly. She told herself it was the position. "For the newlyweds. It's in the cooler."

Wes glanced at the two cuddling honeymooners. "Do you think they're old enough?" he said, his lips quirking, but he went below for the champagne. He pulled the hatch shut before turning on the light in the galley, a courtesy that Lani appreciated since a white light spilling out into the cockpit would make it difficult for her to see into the night that surrounded them. It was another point in his favor; not many people thought to do that.

This is going to work out fine, Lani thought when the light was switched off and he came topside again. *Just fine.* She'd been worried about nothing.

"Here you are." A stemmed plastic glass of champagne appeared under her nose.

Lani looked up to find Wes smiling at her over the bubbling liquid. She shook her head. "Not while I'm working."

"Not even one?"

"No." She looked at the glass in his other hand. "I'd prefer it if you didn't, either."

"Shame to waste it," he said, and then shrugged and tossed the contents of both glasses over the side.

"Thank you."

"You're the boss." His smile widened, turning into that wicked pirate's grin that started her heart to racing. "For now," he warned, and turned to go below again before she could find the words to answer him.

He came back topside a few minutes later with the champagne bottle in one hand and a tray of cold hors d'oeuvres in the other. He offered the tray first, earning a shake of the head from both honeymooners. "Another round, then?" he asked, lifting the champagne bottle.

The bride lifted her glass. "Just a drop more," she said, shooting a coy, sidelong glance at her husband.

"Fill it to the brim," he instructed Wes, reaching out to tip the bottle from the bottom until his wife's glass was full to overflowing. "Drink up, honey," he said, leering. "You know how you get when you've had too much to drink. And you know how much I like it."

His wife giggled and lifted the glass to her lips. Her husband put his hand on her thigh, his fingers just under the hem of her dress.

"Here." Wes handed the bottle to Brad. "I think you'd better take care of this," he said and went to sit beside Lani, leaving the newlyweds as much privacy as possible short of leaving them on deck by themselves.

"Hors d'oeuvre?" he offered blandly, holding the tray in front of Lani.

She picked up a square of papaya that had been rolled in sweetened coconut. Wes selected a cube of cheese.

Brad Jensen growled and pretended to bite his wife's neck. Sheri Jensen giggled and shushed him.

Wes looked over the tray and decided to try a chunk of pineapple next. "This could get embarrassing," he said to

Lani, leaning over the tiller between them to whisper in her ear.

What did he mean, this *could* get embarrassing? Lani thought. It already *was* embarrassing. And bound to get more so, judging from the increasingly intimate attentions of the groom to his bride. Brad Jensen had turned his back on them, but even in the forgiving moonlight it was impossible not to see that he had run one hand up under his wife's dress. The other was tipping more champagne in her glass every time she took a sip.

"He's going to make her sick as a dog," Wes whispered to Lani, shaking his head. "Think I should warn him?"

Lani was staring out over the starboard bow. "No."

"But she's going to pass out on him," Wes insisted, leaning closer. Lani could feel his warm breath on her averted cheek. "Which, believe me, is *not* what he has in mind."

"It's none of your business," Lani hissed.

Wes ignored that. "For what he has in mind, he should have stopped at two glasses. That would be just about enough to loosen her inhibitions nicely without getting her too sloshed to participate in the fun and games."

Lani turned just enough to give him a disgusted look. "I suppose you'd know all about that," she said accusingly, and then clamped her lips shut, realizing how that must have sounded.

Wes grinned wickedly. "Enough," he admitted, and wiggled his eyebrows at her.

Lani's head snapped back to starboard. "Then maybe you ought to take him aside and whisper a few hints before he blows it," she said, forgetting that she'd just told him that it was none of their business.

"Maybe I should," he agreed, putting the hors d'oeuvres tray down on the cushion next to him. He leaned closer, one elbow on the tiller. "But I'd rather sit right here and whisper to you," he said. He was so close that his lips brushed against the hair over her ear, ruffling it as he spoke.

Lani sat very still, hardly breathing, her heart banging against her chest, her blood humming along in her veins, and didn't say a word. Not a word. She couldn't have spoken at that moment if her life had depended on it.

"Actually, I'd like to do a lot more than just whisper," he went on, encouraged by her silence. His voice was a low, husky murmur next to her ear. "Wouldn't you like me to do more than just whisper, Lani?"

She was saved from answering by a high-pitched giggle from the bride. "No, Brad, not here," she admonished, pushing her husband's hand away. "They'll see."

"Too late," Wes said, too low for anyone but Lani to hear, as Brad pulled his wife closer and murmured something in her ear. "We've already seen."

Lani smothered a nervous laugh.

Sheri giggled louder. "Later," she promised, playfully slapping at her husband as she struggled to stand up. Her legs wobbled and she plopped back down. "Oops." She giggled again, then hiccuped. "No more champagne for me," she said wagging her finger at her husband. She was weaving slightly where she sat.

"Maybe you should have something to eat, honey," he suggested, a worried frown creasing his forehead as he steadied her.

"He's seeing his night of wild connubial bliss slipping away from him," Wes muttered.

Lani punched him in the ribs with her elbow.

"Ow," Wes yelped, pretending innocence when the other two occupants of the cockpit turned to look back at them. "What was that for?"

Lani gave him a level look. "Just go below and get the food," she said sternly, trying to hide a smile. "I'm sure Mr. and Mrs. Jensen are ready for something to eat."

Wes snapped to attention as he rose, bringing the heels of his deck shoes together like a well-trained soldier. "Aye, aye, Captain," he said, saluting her before he turned to go below.

"Don't forget the hors d'oeuvres."

"Aye, aye, Captain." He saluted again and picked up the tray of hors d'oeuvres. "Here," he said, handing it to Brad Jensen. "Why don't you and the Mrs. start on these while I dish up the meal?"

Lani's soft laugh followed him into the galley.

The meal was simple but good. Hot black bean soup laced with sherry, cold seafood salad and fresh rolls, with almond cookies and fruit for dessert. Since it had been packaged in four individual boxes, complete with napkins and cutlery, with the soup in small lidded cups, there was little dishing up for Wes to do, aside from setting the coffeepot to perking before he brought everything topside. They were almost through the meal when Wes frowned and glanced up at the sails. "The wind's changed," he said to Lani.

Lani cocked her head, listening. The creaking of the rigging had become less rhythmic and the sails were fluttering very slightly, no longer completely full of wind. Lani adjusted the tiller a bit, then a bit more. "Watch that hot coffee," she warned, holding her own half-full cup aloft to keep it from spilling as the boat heeled.

But even that adjustment wasn't enough. Without thinking about it, she thrust her cup toward Wes, not at all surprised that his hand was there to take it, and shifted to the other side of the tiller. "Coming about," she warned her passengers. "Watch your heads."

The boom swung over the cockpit. The *Wave Dancer* came upright for a moment, as the sails went slack, then obediently heeled over the other way as the wind caught and filled them from the other side. They were tipped low in the water when the maneuver was completed, the sea lapping at the port rail as it rushed by.

Sheri Jensen's eyes were as round as saucers. "What's wrong? Why are we tipped over like this?"

"It's nothing to be worried about," Lani said. "The wind's just picked up a bit, that's all. Remember, I told you it might before we left Ala Wai Harbor?"

"But we're so low in the water!" She clutched at her husband, looking up at Wes for reassurance. "Are we sinking?"

"No, of course not," Wes said soothingly. "There's just a small st—" he started to say "storm," then changed his mind, knowing how that would sound to a frightened landlubber "—a small squall coming in a little earlier than expected, that's all," he told her, returning Lani's surprised look with a small, smug smile. He had checked the weather reports, too. "The winds will get a bit stronger and there might be some small swells. Maybe a white cap or two." He looked up at the night sky. Stars still flickered and the moon glowed softly through wispy, ghostlike clouds. "How long to Lahaina?" he said to Lani.

"Forty minutes. Maybe less."

"Then we'll probably beat the rain," he said to the Jensens as he began gathering up the debris from the meal. "You can go below if you want to," he told them. "But, really, if you don't mind a little wet, you'll have a better time up here."

"Wet!" Sheri seized on that one word. Her hands dug into the front of her husband's shirt. "You mean we're going to have water in here?"

"Just sea spray." Lani kept her voice level, trying hard to contain her excitement. She loved a small storm like this. It was exhilarating. But she knew from experience how easily frightened someone unfamiliar with the sea and its moods could become. "We have plenty of foul-weather gear below," she said, and looked up at Wes to tell him where it was kept. The eyes that looked back at her sparkled with the same suppressed excitement that she was feeling. It was as if she had suddenly found a kindred spirit, someone who felt exactly as she did about the ocean and all her moods. Lani looked away quickly. "It's in the long cupboard next to the head."

"No!" said Sheri as Wes started to go below. "No, I don't want any foul-weather gear. I don't want to stay up here. I want to go below." She grasped her husband's shirtfront tighter. "Brad, I want to go below!" Her words ended on a rising note of panic.

"All right, honey. It's all right," her husband soothed. "We'll go below."

"You're sure?" Wes said as they rose from the cushioned seat in the cockpit. "It's not going to be that bad up here. It probably won't get any worse than it is right now."

"No!" Sheri said before her husband could answer. "I want to go below."

Wes shrugged and stepped back, letting them precede him through the hatchway. The *Wave Dancer* was living up to her name when he came back topside. She skimmed over the small swells whipped up by the wind, sending up a shower of spray with each downward slide of her bow. Lani threw her head back and turned her face into it, loving the feel of the wind and water.

"If they're at all prone to seasickness, they're going to get as sick as dogs down there," Wes said, his feet planted wide for balance. Below decks, as any sailor knew, was the worst place to be in rough weather. Whatever it was that triggered the malady in some people tended to be worse in the confines of the cabin.

"Open the hatch a little so they get some air. That'll help."

We shook his head, automatically grabbing at a line as the *Wave Dancer* pitched sharply. "They don't want air. *She* doesn't want air," he corrected himself, grinning that pirate's grin of his. "I think I heard her say that she wants her mother. Here—" he handed Lani a yellow slicker and motioned her to move over "—put this on. I'll take the tiller for a minute."

Lani shook her head, refusing both the slicker and his offer to man the tiller. "Not unless it starts raining," she said.

It started raining about thirty minutes later, just as they sailed into Lahaina's boat harbor. It was a hard driving rain, but not cold, that plastered their hair to their heads and ran down inside the collars of their slickers as they secured the *Wave Dancer*'s lines to the dock.

Lani slid back the hatch cover enough to poke her head inside. "We're here," she said to the Jensens. "Safe and sound. You can sleep on the boat as you originally planned, or I can arrange for a cab to take you to a hotel." Her inflection made it a question but she already knew what the answer would be. Neither of the two green-tinged faces staring up at her were going to want to spend any more time than absolutely necessary on the boat.

"Hotel," Brad said. Sheri merely nodded, her head resting listlessly against her husband's shoulder.

"I'm sorry the crossing was so rough," Lani said, although it really hadn't been all that bad—unless you'd never been on a sailboat before, she thought, in which case, it had probably been awful. "I hope it hasn't discouraged you from trying sailing another time when it's calmer."

"The hotel," Brad said again.

Lani bit her lip and nodded. "Okay. I'll have to go over to the harbor master's office to make arrangements. If I'm not back, the cab will honk from the end of the dock."

"Fine," Brad said.

Lani slid the hatch closed and jumped to the dock.

"Not coming out?" Wes said, catching her by the arm as she landed.

"Not until their cab gets here." She sighed. "Well, come on. Let's go roust the harbor master."

The lights in the harbor office were on, the harbor master apparently waiting for her. "Hi, Dan," she said, sleeking back her heavy wet hair with both hands. "Got any coffee?"

The gray-haired, bearded man looked up from the airplane model he was putting together on his desk and silently surveyed her. Without a word he rose and disappeared into another room. Lani took off her slicker, motioning at Wes to do the same. She was hanging them both on a coatrack when the harbor master came back into the office with two large towels and two mugs. He tossed the towels at her. "Use these," he said gruffly, turning to fill the mugs with steaming coffee.

Lani handed Wes a towel with a grin and began rubbing the moisture from her hair. Dan's gruffness didn't bother her. An old friend of her father's, Dan had long held the position of a sort of honorary uncle in her life. Doubtless he was, in his silence, preparing one of his speeches. Or rehearsing it more likely. Lani had heard them all.

"Who's this young fella?" he said, handing them each a mug of coffee.

"This is Wes Adams, Gran's lawyer from the mainland. Wes, this is Dan Finlay, an old friend of my father's. And mine," she added, smiling at the older man.

"Humph," he snorted, and turned his back on them, re-seating himself behind his desk. Wes and Lani stood where he left them, mugs in hand. "Well, sit," he barked, motion-ing at the two wooden chairs in front of his desk. "No call to be looming over a body like a pair of half-drowned vul-tures."

They sat. Lowering her eyes, Lani lifted the steaming mug of coffee to her lips and prepared to listen. She knew from experience that Dan had to have his say before anyone else could have theirs.

"That meek look won't do you any good, my girl," he growled.

Lani dropped the pretense and grinned at him.

"Nor will any of your minx's tricks work. You've been a thoughtless, reckless girl...."

She could have almost said it herself, word for word, but she sipped her coffee instead and tried to look properly re-pentant. Wes did the same, minus the repentant look. His expression, as he looked back and forth between the rain-soaked water sprite sitting next to him and the crusty old sea dog across the desk, said he was enjoying himself im-mensely.

"...and have you no more brains," Dan fairly thun-dered, "than to head out in a storm?"

"It wasn't a storm when we started out." She looked at the man beside her for confirmation. "Was it, Wes?"

"Don't get me involved in this," he said, and buried his nose in his coffee cup.

She gave him a disgusted look. "Well, it wasn't," she in-sisted, turning back to Dan. "And it isn't one now, not really."

"Small craft warnings went up fifteen minutes ago."

"There, you see?" she pointed out, her smile triumph-ant. "We were already in port fifteen minutes ago."

"Nitpicking, my girl." Dan shook his head sadly, but there was an answering smile beneath his beard. "You're just like your father. God rest his soul."

The lecture was over.

Lani swallowed the last of her coffee and put the empty mug on the edge of Dan's desk. "Back to work," she said, standing. "I've got two passengers, Dan, and they need a room for tonight. They don't want to spend any more time on the *Wave Dancer* than absolutely necessary."

"What about this fella?" Dan nodded at Wes.

"Oh, he's not a passenger. He's crew. He came over to take a look at some ketch that's for sale. A forty-five footer, didn't you say, Wes?"

"I don't know of any forty-five-foot ketch for sale," Dan said before Wes could answer. "No ketches at all, come to think of it. The McCarthys are selling their little sloop. Sue's having a baby and they've decided it's time to settle down." He scratched his beard. "Old Jack Cho's been talking about gettin' rid of that old cat of his again. But a ketch?" He shook his head slowly. "You sure it was a ketch, young fella? Anchored here in Lahaina?"

Wes rose and set his coffee cup on the desk. There was a half-sheepish, half-sly look on his face. "Well, actually," he glanced over at Lani, knowing there was nothing to do now but confess and take whatever punishment she meted out like a man. And mete it out, she would. He had no doubt about that. "There isn't any ketch."

Lani stared at him. "No ketch?"

He nodded solemnly. "No ketch."

"Well, then, why did you tell me there was?" She paused for a moment, gathering her thoughts, wondering what that teasing gleam in his blue eyes meant. "How come you wanted to come on this cruise, then?"

Wes shoved his hands into the pockets of his damp white pants. "I just wanted to see what kind of sailor you are," he said, shrugging.

"And?" she said. Her tone was frosty.

"And you're not bad," he complimented her, then glanced at Dan and winked. "For a woman."

Both men burst into sudden, delighted laughter at her outraged expression.

She stood there for a moment, her narrowed gaze flickering back and forth between the two men. One of them a lifelong friend, the other someone she had actually thought about kissing again. Both of them chuckling over his little joke like a pair of jackals! Well, she'd see who had the last laugh.

"If you find that so amusing," she said, "let's see how funny it is when you have to get back to Oahu on your own."

The door of the harbor office rattled when she slammed it behind her.

8

WHEN LANI SAILED into Ala Wai Harbor the next afternoon it was almost five o'clock. Securing the *Wave Dancer*'s lines but not bothering with any cleanup beyond stuffing the paper debris into a garbage bag, she hurried over to the Sail Away office. The bamboo shade on the plate-glass window was partially pulled down, the door was locked, and Lani couldn't find her keys in either pocket of her shorts. She must have dropped them in the cabin of the boat, she decided, when she undressed last night. Stifling a scream of pure frustration, she went back for them. Fifteen minutes later she returned, keys in hand, and let herself into the office.

Where was Kim, she wondered, flicking on the overhead light with an annoyed snap. The teenager was supposed to stay until six and it wasn't quite five-thirty. Come to think of it, where was Rich? Hell, where was anyone?

Lani moved behind her desk and dropped heavily into the captain's chair. The top was littered with telephone messages, a half-empty can of soda and several teen magazines. The boyish face of the latest teen idol grinned up at her from no less than three of the covers.

Lani grinned wearily back at him and pushed them aside, reaching for the messages. There were several from Al Duffy, sounding irate, and one from her grandmother, asking that she call home. Rich had checked in and left a number where he could be reached "in an emergency." There were several more from people whose names Lani didn't recognize and, on the bottom, one from Kim herself.

I quit, read Lani in astonishment. *The phone doesn't stop ringing. People yell at me. I don't know where anyone is. So I quit!!* Underneath her signature Kim had added a short P.S. *Sorry.*

"Great," Lani said, tossing the pink slip down. "This is just great!" She folded both arms on top of the desk and lowered her head onto them. It was, she decided, a perfectly awful ending to a perfectly awful day.

She'd had to hang around Lahaina all morning and a good portion of the afternoon, waiting for the small craft warnings to be rescinded. She might have left anyway, despite the warnings, but Dan would have worried himself sick until he heard she was safe. And he'd have called her grandmother, too, to let her know that Lani had disregarded the safety precautions. And that would have meant no end of recriminations when she finally got home. So Lani had waited, leaving the second the warning flag was lowered.

The sail back to Ala Wai had been uneventful. She had pushed the *Wave Dancer* as hard as she dared, heeling her way over, feeling the wind and the salt spray sting her face. But even that had failed to lift her mood.

And now this.

Kim had walked out before the end of a working day, just quit because the phone kept ringing! And, to top it off, she'd forgotten to switch on the answering machine when she'd left. Or maybe she'd done it deliberately. As revenge.

"Who knows?" Lani said dispiritedly. "Who cares?"

She certainly didn't. Not at the moment, anyway. At the moment she wondered why she was even trying to run this business. She certainly wasn't having any fun. And it had always been fun when her father was alive. But all she'd had to do then was go sailing. Now she spent most of her time worrying about invoices and other unpleasant things.

Maybe her grandmother was right. Maybe she should turn the whole thing over to someone else and let them worry about it, she thought.

"And I could go back to sailing all day," she mumbled into her folded arms, feeling thoroughly put upon and sorry for herself. "No responsibilities. No bookkeeping chores. No reason not to get involved with a man." She heard the door open. "Go away," she said without raising her head. "We're closed."

"Sleeping on the job?" asked an amused male voice.

Lani lifted her head just enough to peer over her folded arms. Wes Adams stood just inside the office door, one hand still on the knob, looking as fresh and vital as if it were the beginning of a long day rather than the end of one. He'd obviously made it back to Oahu without a hitch, she thought sourly, thoroughly regretting the twinge of remorse she'd felt about leaving him to fend for himself. Thank goodness it had been just a twinge. She'd hated to have wasted time feeling guilty over nothing. She laid her head back down on her arms. "Go away," she said again.

Wes just laughed. She heard the door close and the soft sound of his steps as he crossed to her desk, the protesting creak of the canvas and wood chair as he lowered himself into it. Then, nothing.

Well, go ahead—gloat, she thought, refusing to look up and see him grinning at her.

His words, when they came, were almost worse than having him crow over her. "Tough day?" he said sympathetically.

But Lani wasn't in the mood for sympathy, especially not from him. She lifted her head and glared at him. "What do you want?" she said rudely.

He grinned at her. "I came to give you a lift home."

"I don't need a lift home. I have the Jeep, remember?"

Wes shook his head. "Your friend Rich has the Jeep," he said, smiling into her narrowed eyes. He clasped his hands behind his head and leaned back, thoroughly at ease and enjoying himself. "He stopped by Walsh Imports today to ask if I'd mind picking you up. We had an interesting talk," he added, but didn't elaborate. His right eyebrow quirked upward, waiting for her to ask.

She was dying to know just what they'd talked about but refused to give him the satisfaction of asking. "And do you?" she asked instead.

The eyebrow stayed raised.

"Mind picking me up," she elaborated.

"Not at all." He dropped his hands, rose from the chair and walked over to the door with that sexy roll in his narrow hips that was almost a swagger. "Coming?" he asked politely, his hand on the doorknob.

Lani hesitated for a second. It would give her a great deal of satisfaction to refuse the ride home, to say "No, thank you. I can manage," as he had managed when she'd left him stranded on Maui. But Rich, curse and rot him, had taken the Jeep again and she couldn't manage, not unless she called a taxi or rented a car. Which was a tempting but stupid thought, really, when a ride home was standing right in front of her. But damn, she hated giving in like this!

"Moonmaid?"

"Yes, I'm coming," she said irritably. Sighing, she flipped on the answering machine and locked up, trailing after him to her grandmother's late-model Mercedes, all the while consoling herself with the thought of a long, hot soak in the *furo* and a steaming cup of Fomi's sweet, green tea.

LANI MAINTAINED A STUBBORN silence on the way home, answering Wes's casual comments with monosyllables until, with a maddening, lighthearted shrug, he gave up and concentrated on the powerful car he was driving and the curving road to her grandmother's house.

He drove well, Lani noticed, stealing looks at him from under lowered lashes. His hands rested lightly on the wheel, strong and square, with long fingers and neatly manicured nails. He wore an expensive watch made of some brushed silver metal on his left wrist and a ring with a small jade stone on the ring finger of his right hand. He had his suit coat off again, the sleeves of his white shirt rolled halfway up his forearms. She could see the individual hairs that grew there, gold against his tanned skin. His citrusy after-shave teased at her nose. He was humming, off key, along with the rock song on the radio, tapping his ring against the steering wheel in time with the music.

Her eyes traveled slowly upward, unconsciously caressing his muscled shoulders and strong brown throat, coming to rest, at last, on his profile. He had the nose of a man who wasn't afraid of sticking it where it might not belong, she thought admiringly. And a chin that said he could handle whatever consequences his curiosity might bring. Then there was that crooked little scar that curled over and under his jaw, silently hinting at past adventures. His lips were curved upward, smiling faintly, almost arrogantly, she thought, as if he were aware of her scrutiny. And pleased by it.

Lani hastily averted her eyes, focusing blindly on the passing scenery, and refused to look at him again.

Wes's grin got wider.

The big car had barely pulled to a stop in front of the house before Lani was out and running lightly up the steps. Fomi opened the door as she reached it and Lani, request-

ing that tea be brought to her in the *furo*, hurriedly kicked
off her sneakers and headed for the safety of her room.

She could hear Wes's low tones and Fomi's answering
giggles and, seconds later, the soft musical voice of Sumiko
asking a question. It was Wes who answered her, his tone
reassuring, and then Lani heard him coming down the hall,
humming the rock song that had been playing on the car
radio. The door slid open to his room.

Lani waited a minute, holding her breath, expecting to
hear Sumiko's soft footsteps come padding along behind
him, but there was no sound. She let out her breath and
headed for the shower.

Dropping her clothes to the tiled floor, she turned the taps
on full force, rapidly filling the small bathroom with a cloud
of steam. She shampooed her hair twice, ridding it of all
traces of salt and sea air, smiling a little as she recalled a
scene from the old movie, *South Pacific*, where the heroine
"washed that man right out of her hair." The only thing was,
she remembered, slicking her hair back with her hands as
she rinsed the soap out and found Wes still lurking on the
edges of her mind, it hadn't worked in the movie, either. She
made a face at the mirror and reached for her terry robe.
Barefoot, with her wet hair slicked back and her tanned face
free of makeup, she slid open her door to peer cautiously
down the hall before heading for the *furo*.

The small, steamy room was basically Japanese, with a
few Western touches added. The floor was tiled, with a drain
in the center for easy cleaning. The walls were paneled with
natural unfinished wood. Six ceramic hooks were spaced
along one wall with an open shelf stacked with fluffy white
towels above them and a wooden bench below. The lighting was low and restful. And, instead of the small stools and
buckets of warm water where it was traditional to sit and

wash oneself before entering the soaking tub, Edward Walsh had installed a shower.

The tub itself stood in the center of the room, approximately six feet square, smooth molded fiberglass inside, with a wide wooden edge all around. It was deep enough at one end to cover the shoulders of a tall man sitting upright. Fomi had already folded back the wooden cover that kept the water hot and steam rose in lazy spirals from the still surface.

Lani removed her robe, hanging it on a hook, and slowly eased herself into the steaming water until it covered her breasts. With a satisfied sigh she closed her eyes, leaning her head back on the edge of the tub, feeling her muscles uncoil, one by one, as the water drew the tension from her body. You could keep all the saunas and steam rooms in the world, she thought contentedly; there was nothing like a good, long soak in a steaming *furo* to put things in their proper perspective. After she had been soothed by the tranquil atmosphere of the *furo*, she always felt relaxed and renewed, well able to take on whatever problems had seemed insurmountable before.

She sank lower, letting the caressing water and dim, restful quietness of the room work their magic, falling into a light sleep for a few moments. Fomi, she knew, would rouse her before she had soaked too long.

Her mind barely registered the sound of the door sliding open nor the light footfalls approaching the tub. There was a soft click of wood against wood, a slight stirring of the warm air near her. Fomi with her tea, she thought lazily. Without opening her eyes, she languidly lifted her arm out of the water to accept it. Small droplets slithered over her smooth skin, plopping soundlessly into the tub. A small, handleless, heated cup was pressed into her palm. She brought it to her lips, lifting her head slightly to sip the fragrant brew. It was exactly as she liked it—hot and sweet.

"Mmm. *Mahalo*, Fomi," she said, opening her eyes to place the cup back on the tray beside the tub. A hair-dusted shin was directly in her line of vision.

"You're welcome," Wes said, grinning that pirate's grin of his.

Lani gasped. The cup slipped from her wet fingers, spilling tea across the tray. "Where's Fomi?" she demanded, sinking lower in the tub and crossing her arms over her breasts. Her knees jackknifed, automatically concealing her lower body.

"Fomi's in the kitchen, I imagine, seeing to dinner." He crouched easily by the tub, clad in a navy batik-print *yukata* that sagged open across his bare, hair-covered chest and dipped down between his thighs, calmly wiping up the spilled tea with a small towel. "At least, that's where she said she'd be when I met her in the hall a few minutes ago and relieved her of the tea tray." He righted her teacup. "Would you like another?"

"No, I would not like another," she snapped, her eyes focused just above the carelessly tied blue knot on the sash of his cotton robe. To look up would be to see that tempting wedge of his wide, golden-haired chest. To look down would be to see his naked knees and calves and that same golden hair dusting the inside of his right thigh where the robe fell away. "I would like you to please leave."

"But I was planning on having a soak before dinner. That is—" he added, his right eyebrow lifting mockingly "—unless it would make you uncomfortable."

"No, of course not," she lied, determined to match his urbane casualness. A difficult feat, at best, when she sat with her arms crossed over her breasts and her knees pulled up practically to her chin. She relaxed her knees and tried

to rearrange her arms so that the posture looked more natural. "We Japanese don't have the same hang-ups about
nudity as you Westerners do," she said, lifting one shoulder in what she hoped was a careless shrug. Her eyes were
still fastened on the knot of his *yukata*.

Wes grinned. "Good. Then I won't have to forego a soak."
He refilled her cup, setting it within reach, then poured one
for himself. "Two of my favorite Japanese traditions," he
said, sipping the tea. "Hot tea and the communal bath." He
reached out and casually tucked a wayward strand of wet
hair behind her ear. It was as soft and sleek as a wet satin
ribbon and his fingers lingered, moving down to trail over
her jawline. They came to rest just under her chin, urging
her to lift her face to his. "The lovely geisha is an added
plus," he said teasingly.

Lani refused to meet his eyes but she didn't jerk away. "I'm
not a geisha," she said, trying desperately to keep her voice
from shaking as much as her insides were. Her wet lashes
fluttered slightly against her cheeks. "A geisha is a profes-
sional hostess. She's rigor . . . rigorously trained in conversation and . . . ah, food service. She, ah, she . . ." What was
it a geisha was trained to do? "She's trained in traditional,
ah, singing and . . ." Oh, what did it matter? Unable to stop
herself, Lani lifted her eyes to his. "I'm not a geisha," she repeated softly, as if it were important.

Wes was caught. Caught and held by the hesitant, hungry look in her wide eyes. "Lovely, enchanting moonmaid,
then," he murmured, mesmerized. With her face damp and
free of makeup, her hair slicked back, her skin flushed, she
looked delicate and strong, ethereal and disturbingly sensual all at once.

All casualness, all intent to tease her, vanished. He could
feel his heart beating, pulsating in his fingertips. And his
hand was actually trembling against her chin—trembling

over something so simple, so previously asexual, as the feel of her chin against his fingers! Slowly, experimentally, he moved them down the slender column of her throat, feeling the sleek, wet smoothness of her tanned skin.

Lani's lips parted on a small, indrawn breath. Her head fell back a bit. But her eyes still held his, unable to look away. Still hungry but less hesitant now.

He moved his trembling fingertips a bit lower, across her fragile collarbone, tracing it, dipping into the vulnerable little hollows above and below. She was so soft. So smooth. His eyes left hers to follow the path of his fingertips as they traced the gentle upper curve of her breasts, which were partially revealed by the water and her crossed arms.

She was like sun-warmed silk, he thought, marveling at the texture and delicacy of her wet skin. Softer and warmer than every soft, warm thing he had ever touched. And how she burned him! The heat of her seemed to race from his fingertips, up his arm and down again, until he was on fire for her.

Lani held herself stock-still, not daring to move, scarcely daring to breath, feeling tiny, darting sparks wherever his fingers touched her. A feeling of anticipation and dread coiled in the pit of her stomach as his fingers dipped below the water. Heat ricocheted through her, flaring into excitement as his thumb brushed over her nipple. It seared her nerve endings, making her want him with an intensity that frightened her. Damn him and his blue eyes and his rakish pirate's grin and his talented touch!

She had to do something to stop this, she thought desperately. *Now,* before it went any further. She roused herself with an effort, shaking off the drugging sensation that his touch had created. Lifting her arm from the water, she slapped his hand away.

"If you're going to soak in the *furo*, then soak," she said, scowling fiercely to hide the trembling still going on inside her. "But don't think that just because we have communal bathing in this house, it means you can play sneaky touchie-feelie games."

Wes sat back on his heels and stared at her, openmouthed. What the hell had happened? One minute she was sitting there, trembling under his hand, practically eating him with those huge black eyes of hers, and the next she was accusing him of being some kind of pervert. Sneaky touchie-feelie games, indeed, he thought, insulted. He didn't need to play sneaky, adolescent games. He was past that sort of thing. Unless they were mutual, of course. And he'd thought they were.

"Get in or get out," Lani snapped, still fighting the insane urge to reach up and drag him into the water on top of her. "But don't crouch there staring at me as if you were at some peep show."

Peep show? He'd show her a peep show, all right. He stood. "I have to shower first," he bit out, already shrugging out of his *yukata*.

Lani clamped her eyes shut and then, unable to resist, opened them a crack, earning herself a peek at his broad bare back, his long, hard-muscled hairy legs and his pale, untanned rear end as he stepped into the shower and banged the door closed behind him.

WES TURNED THE COLD WATER on himself full force and leaned into it, his hands braced on the tiled wall in front of him as it pounded down on his head. Of all the stupid things to do, he railed at himself. He had no more meant to get into that tub with her than he had meant to touch her in the first place. He'd only meant to tease her a bit, see if he could make her blush, please himself by looking at her a little. A little experiment, so to speak, to see if what had happened the other morning on the lanai was just a crazy fluke, or if it would happen again when they were close and alone.

They were in her grandmother's house, after all. Hardly the place for a full-fledged seduction, even if that's what he'd been planning when he brought the tea in to her. Which, he swore to himself, he hadn't.

And then, somehow, it had all gotten out of hand. He had touched her and his control had slipped the leash, and he was left standing in the shower, buck naked and as aroused as he had ever been in his life, with the focus of that arousal waiting for him to join her in the *furo*. He gritted his teeth and raised his head, pushing away from the shower wall to let the icy needles of water hit him where it would be most effective. He hoped.

Outside in the *furo*, Lani sat in the steaming water and wondered whether she could get out of the tub, into her robe and out of the room before he got out of the shower. Or would he open the door as she was fleeing and catch an undignified glimpse of her bare bottom as she had his?

Better to stay where she was, she decided, keeping her eyes averted from his blurred image behind the frosted glass of the shower stall. Better for her dignity. Better for her pride. She'd said that it wouldn't bother her if he shared the *furo*, that the Japanese didn't have the same hang-ups as Westerners did about nudity. Never mind that she was more Western than Japanese herself, or that she'd never shared the *furo* with anyone but family. Oh, hell, maybe retreat was the best idea after all—pride and dignity be damned. She rose halfway out of the tub, prepared to make a dash for it.

The shower spray stopped. The shower door creaked open. Slowly, very slowly, but Lani wasn't aware of that.

Too late, she thought, sitting back down with a splash. Her retreat had been cut off. She averted her head and picked up her teacup, practically burying her nose in it. After all, she reasoned, having no hang-ups about nudity didn't mean that you stared at naked men while they got into the tub.

Damn, still there, Wes thought, eyeing her from behind the half-open shower door. He'd stayed in there long enough to give her time to get out but she hadn't moved. She was still sitting in the water, cool as you please, sipping tea as if both of them weren't as naked as babies. Trying to show him up, probably, and he'd be damned if he was going to let her do that. He would show her that her nudity didn't bother him any more than his did her. Oh, hell, he thought, disgusted with himself, it was a load of malarkey because, in any case, it bothered him. A lot. Feeling like a total fool for making such a big deal over a little bare flesh, he left the relative security of the shower and headed for the *furo.*

Lani heard the soft splash of water as he lowered himself into the water and tipped her teacup higher, draining it. When she lowered the cup, Wes was sitting across from her, chest deep in the water, a grimace twisting his mouth.

"Too hot?" she said, smirking.

After the cold shower it felt like he was being boiled alive. "No," he said, and forced himself to smile. "Mind passing me my tea?"

"Not at all." Lani picked up his cup from the tray and held out her arm. He held out his. Three or so inches of space still separated their hands. She leaned forward. He leaned forward. Their eyes touched, flared, looked away. He took the cup of tea and they both scooted back into their respective corners.

He sipped at the lukewarm liquid. The cold shower hadn't done any good, dammit. Or, more precisely, it had, but then she'd leaned forward like that, her arm outstretched, her small, sweet breasts with their small, dark nipples visible under the still water, her fragrance intensified by the hot steam, and it hadn't made any difference that he'd just tried to freeze his private parts.

What did you say to a naked woman, he wondered, when you weren't about to make love to her, or weren't actually making love to her, or hadn't just finished making love to her? What was the polite thing to do when you found yourself, mostly through your own stupidity, alone in a tub the size of a playpen with a sensual watersprite of a woman and your blood was pumping like crazy and you knew hers was, too, but neither of you were going to do anything about it?

"I suppose Fomi will have dinner ready soon," he said, and wondered just how the hell he was going to get out of the tub without exposing all he was feeling to the woman sitting across from him.

"Yes, I suppose she will," Lani answered, wondering if she could force herself to just stand up and get out and get it over with. She wouldn't have to look at him while she did it, and it would be over in a few minutes. She could just turn her back, get out and get her robe. But she continued to sit there, fiddling with her empty cup, keeping her forearms bent in front of her, unable to make herself do it.

Peeking at him from under her lashes, she could see his flat, masculine nipples through the still, steamy water. His navel was less clear, the narrow line of hair bisecting his lean midriff barely visible. The area below his waist was, thankfully, shadowy and indistinct. It stood to reason that he could probably see that much of her, too, if he looked. And she knew he'd looked. She drew her knees up a bit higher and fixed her gaze on the empty cup in her hands.

Maybe she should just ask him to close his eyes while she got out. "Does the water temperature feel more comfortable now?" she asked, unable to think of anything else—unable to continue sitting there in tongue-tied silence.

"Yes, fine," he answered, wondering if he should just turn his back and get out. After all, she'd already seen his bare buns, so what harm could it do? Except, of course, to his ego. But if he stayed in the tub much longer, he'd either be permanently poached or he'd give in to his baser instincts and jump on her.

He eyed her speculatively, sitting there with her sleek, wet head bent over that teacup. What would she do if he gave in to his baser instincts?

He wouldn't find out now—Fomi had just come in.

"Ah, Missy Lani, you stay so long in the *furo*, you be all wrinkled up," she said, bustling over to where the towels were stacked. "Come, now. Get out." She shook out a towel and held it up between her wide-spread arms, waiting for Lani to do as she was bid. "Come, come," she chided. "You get out now. Dinner be soon. You must hurry and make ready."

Lani looked over at Wes. He was watching her, making no effort to pretend he wasn't, waiting to see what she would do. His eyes were blue flame, full of speculation and anticipation and pure masculine desire. There was a challenge, too, in this teasing, devil-may-care gleam. *I dare you*, his eyes said.

Lani rose to the dare. Literally. She came up out of the *furo* like Venus rising from the sea. Water streamed from her straight, shapely shoulders and down over her small, firm breasts. It dripped from her pebbled nipples and caressed her narrow waist. It slid over her slender hips and through the thatch of jet black hair at the apex of her legs, and ran down her thighs to the tub. She stood there for a moment or two, letting him look his fill, and then she turned, an empress dismissing the masses, and stepped out of the tub, letting Fomi enfold her in the towel, all the while hoping that neither of them could see how much she was shaking.

Wes gulped and wondered if it would be too obvious if he crossed his legs.

"There, you get dry now, Missy Lani," Fomi said, releasing the towel as Lani held it to her. She pushed her charge gently toward the door, then stooped, bending at the knees to pick up the tea tray. "Mrs. Walsh-san say that you are please to spend as much time as you like," she said, giggling at Wes as she straightened. "*Furo* relax you much, you see," she promised, bowing as she slid the door closed and left him alone.

Relax, hell, thought Wes.

9

LANI WENT TO BED early, declining dinner with the not entirely fabricated excuse of a headache. And then she lay there, twisting and turning restlessly on the *futon*, punching at her pillow, staring at the ceiling, trying to get comfortable, trying to banish the unsettling feelings that had followed her from the *furo* to her bedroom.

But banishment was impossible; the best she could do was try to rationalize them away, take them out and examine them and hope, somehow, to make them less disturbing.

It all boiled down to one simple thing, really. Physical attraction—an emotion based on hormones and propinquity and that undefinable thing known as chemistry. It was nothing new to her, of course, not at twenty-five years old, except in degree. She had never wanted someone as intensely, as fiercely as she wanted Wesley Adams, attorney-at-law. But did she dare to consider forgetting everything that counseled her against involvement with him?

Reason said no. He was her grandmother's lawyer, for one thing. A conflict of interest if there ever was one. And she simply didn't have time for a relationship of any kind at this point in her life, not with everything else that was going on. She didn't *want* a relationship right now.

Did she?

No, she told herself firmly, pulling the pillow over her head to block out the image of him, naked and wet and magnificent in the steaming water of the *furo*. But it was no use. Other images replaced it, kaleidoscoping through her mind in a relentless, dizzying parade. Wes flashing that maddening, irresistible pirate's grin of his as he teased her... his blue eyes meeting hers across the width of the *Wave Dancer*'s cockpit, full of excitement at the approach of rough weather... his right eyebrow lifted to register a question or deliver a teasing comment... his muscular forearms, bared by the rolled-back cuffs of his shirt-sleeves... his face as he bent down to kiss her that morning on the lanai... his hand touching her breasts in the *furo*.

"No!" she said aloud, her voice muffled by the pillow. She *wasn't* interested. She *wouldn't* get involved.

She punched the pillow and rolled over, then rolled over and punched it again. It didn't help. She couldn't sleep. She couldn't even lie still! Her mind was full of wicked fantasies; her body was full of churning desires. What she needed was a rousing, rough sail, or a mile-long swim or— Oh, God, what she needed was him!

She sat up, threw her cover off and rose from the *futon*, heading out into the night. She'd sit beside the *koi* pond for a while and watch the fish. Maybe that would relax her.

She almost stumbled over Wes sitting on the edge of the lanai. He had an ashtray balanced on his bent knee, a cheroot clenched between his teeth, and an expression of wariness and voracious hunger in his eyes as he looked up at her.

She sat down on the step beside him, drew her knees up and wrapped her arms around her bare legs. "I can't sleep," she said, staring out into the shadowed garden.

"Neither can I."

"What are we going to do about it?" she asked quietly.

"What do you want to do about it?"

Lani took a deep breath and turned her head toward him. "I want to go to bed with you."

Wes felt his breathing stop. "Now?"

"Yes." The word was barely audible.

Very deliberately Wes crushed out his cheroot. Setting the ashtray aside, he stood and held out his hand. Lani put hers into it and he pulled her to her feet. Without another word they turned and walked through the open door into his room, stopping at the foot of the *futon*.

Still holding her hand, Wes bent his head and kissed her softly. "Wait here a minute." He put his finger to her lips as she opened her mouth to speak. "For just one minute." He disappeared into the bathroom, coming out with a small toiletry case that he dropped on the floor beside the *futon*.

They stood there for another long, silent moment, facing each other in the moonlit darkness. The sweet scents of the tropical night surrounded them. The rhythm of their breathing filled their ears. The heat of their desire for each other filled the small space between their bodies, becoming hotter and more intense with each second that they held it at bay.

And then Lani reached out and lowered the zipper of his jeans. "This isn't going to change anything," she warned him—and herself.

Wes pushed the narrow straps of her camisole down her arms. "I know."

"It's only physical desire." She touched the bare, hair-dusted flesh of his lower belly. It was hard and warm. "Only passion."

"Yes," he said, cupping her breasts. Her nipples were like pearls against his palms. "Only passion."

"I haven't got time for a relationship," she whispered. Her breathing was ragged. Her breasts ached with the sweetness of his touch. "I don't want a relationship."

"No," Wes agreed. "Neither do I." He reached down and pushed her hand lower inside his jeans. "Touch me."

She curled her fingers around him. He was hot and hard. "Only physical desire," she said again as if it were desperately important that they both understand that.

Wes groaned and pushed his jeans all the way down, kicking them off when they reached his feet. He reached for her again, skimming his hands down her torso and under the silky camisole that was bunched around her waist. "Only desire," he murmured, slipping his hands into the elastic waist of her tap pants. He pushed the material down her legs to the floor, his fingers sliding over the curve of her hips and then back up to the soft hair at the juncture of her thighs. "But this is so good," he said, pressing his palm against the soft folds of her.

Lani's knees buckled and she collapsed against him like a rag doll. He caught her and, together, they fell to the rumpled *futon*. They pressed close for a long, burning moment, relishing the feel of flesh against flesh.

And then Wes drew away slightly, supporting himself on an elbow, and looked down into her face. He could barely see her in the shadowed moonlight that filtered into the room—the gleam of her passion-glazed eyes, the shine of her lips where she had licked them, that was all. But she was utterly beautiful, completely desirable and he had never wanted a woman more. "Lani," he murmured hoarsely. "Lani, my sweet."

"No, don't talk," she whispered. There was a frantic edge to her voice. "Don't talk. Just love me."

"I will." His lips brushed against hers. "I do."

"Now." She tugged at his shoulders. Her hips rocked against him. "Now."

"Yes." He reached sideways for the toiletry case he'd brought in from the bathroom. A moment later he was lifting himself over her, searching for her body's opening. "Now," he said, sliding at last into the heated nest between her thighs. What little breath he had left hissed out between his teeth. She was so hot. So wet. So welcoming. "Lani."

"Yes," she whimpered, bucking against him. "Yes. Yes. Yes." The word became a mindless chant, uttered in time to his thrusts. Faster and faster. Deeper and harder. Her back arched, her pelvis tilted and she went as taut as a sail in a gale-force wind. "*Yes,*" she screamed softly, biting down on her bottom lip to hold back the sound.

Wes went wild, his body driving mindlessly toward his own release, plunging into the woman beneath him. He crested a moment later, driving Lani over the top for a second time as he groaned and stiffened in her arms.

The whole thing had taken less than ten minutes—ten glorious, exhausting, exhilarating minutes that contained more passion than either of them had ever know before.

"Lani," he murmured into her neck, wanting to say, needing to say. . . something.

"Don't talk," she said groggily, tightening her arms around his neck. "Don't talk. Just hold me."

He wrapped his arms more securely around her and rolled to his side. Utterly replete, they slept.

LANI WOKE EARLY the next morning in her own bed, feeling deliciously relaxed and refreshed without knowing quite why. She stretched luxuriously and thoroughly, like a cat after a long nap in the sun, pleasantly aware of the "thrump-thrump" of a hand-powered lawn mower and the snip of garden shears just outside her room. The morning breeze billowed the curtains at her window, and she turned toward them, her eyes following the long buttery fingers of sunlight that filtered into the room to where they tiptoed across the foot of her bed. A jumble of silky material glimmered softly in the light. Her camisole and tap pants.

Lani froze in midstretch, the previous night rushing back to her in full force. That's why she felt so refreshed this morning. So satisfied. The ache of unfulfilled desire was gone. She had gone to Wes—gone *looking* for him in the night—and they had made love.

No, she corrected herself, sitting up, they had had sex. There would be no dressing it up in pretty words. They had, in plain English, had sex.

She covered her face with her hands. *Oh, God, what was she going to do now? How was she going to face him? How would she act? What would she say?*

She jumped up, grabbing her nightclothes from the foot of the bed, and headed for the bathroom. Avoiding her reflection in the mirror, she stuffed the camisole and tap pants into the laundry hamper and stepped into the shower.

It wasn't that she actually regretted what had happened between them last night, she thought, standing there under the stinging spray. It would be impossible for her to regret what had been one of the most emotionally intense, most physically satisfying experiences of her life. It was just that she felt as if she'd revealed far too much of herself, too soon—as if she'd opened herself emotionally to something she wasn't ready for.

She needed time to sort it out. Time to put the experience in its proper perspective before she saw him again. She needed time to decide how she was going to act, what she was going to say or do. She needed time to think things through.

"Or not to think at all," she said aloud, reaching for the blow-dryer to do her hair.

Fifteen minutes later she was heading stealthily down the hall to the front door.

"Granddaughter," said Sumiko from somewhere behind her.

Lani barely turned around. "Yes, Gran? What is it?"

Sumiko frowned at her impatient tone. "I merely wish to bid you good morning," she said with a touch of asperity. "And to inquire after your health."

"My health?"

"You were not at dinner, Granddaughter. A headache, I believe Fomi said."

"Yes, well, it wasn't a headache, exactly." Lani tucked her arm into her grandmother's and propelled her down the hall to the foyer. No sense waking Wes up at such an early hour. He probably needed his sleep after last night. Lani felt herself flushing and pushed the thought away. "I was just, ah, tired, that's all," she told Sumiko, "and I wouldn't have been very good company."

"Still, we have a guest, Granddaughter. Or have you forgotten?"

Lani shook her head. Forgotten Wes? She only wished she could!

"It was most distressing to me that your place at dinner should be vacant simply because you do not feel like putting in an appearance. It is an example of these modern, heedless manners," Sumiko said as Lani sat down to put on her Topsiders. "And it does not do honor to our house, Granddaughter."

Lani looked up. "I'm sorry, Gran," she said, meaning it sincerely. The honor of her house and family meant a great deal to Sumiko. "I didn't mean to upset you. I didn't think."

Sumiko nodded, satisfied that her granddaughter's remorse was real, if not as deep as she would have liked. "You will offer your apologies to Wesley, also, and we will say no more about it."

"Offer my apologies?" Lani sputtered, breaking off as Sumiko reached out and stroked her hair softly.

"It is understandable, of course," Sumiko said, brushing the gleaming strands back from her granddaughter's face. "You are little more than a girl still, and must be expected to be heedless and headstrong at times."

Oh, Gran, if you only knew how heedless I've been!

Sumiko's hand fell back to her side. "I was such as you, when I was a girl."

"You, Gran?" Lani's voice was frankly skeptical. Sumiko was the most self-controlled woman she knew.

"Yes, even I." A reminiscent smile touched her aged eyes, lighting them for a moment. "But that is not important now," she said briskly, shaking away the brief memory. "What is important, Granddaughter, is that you apologize to our guest for your rudeness at the earliest opportunity."

"Yes, Gran," Lani said meekly. *In a pig's eye.*

Thirty minutes later Lani was standing outside the Sail Away office, digging through her canvas tote for the keys to open the door. But the keys proved unnecessary. The door was already open, the lock not quite latched.

"Rich?" she said hopefully, pushing open the door. "Is that you?"

The figure at the file cabinet straightened suddenly, slamming the metal door shut. "No." The voice was hesitant, a bit breathless. "It's me. Kim."

"Kim? What are you doing here in this gloom?" Lani dropped her canvas bag on a chair and went to raise the bamboo shade on the window. "There, that's better." She turned back to the girl still standing beside the file cabinet. "I thought you quit?"

"Well, I did, but . . ." Kim clasped her hands together, twisting them in front of her. Her eyes were downcast, her cheeks flushed. "What I mean is, ah, I'm sorry about yesterday. Leaving and—" she lifted her hands in a fluttery little gesture "—everything. I know I shouldn't have but it got so crazy around here and, well, I, um, just freaked out, I guess." Her eyes met Lani's fleetingly before skittering away again. "I promise not to do it again, if you'll hire me back."

"Well, I—"

"I promise, Lani," she said. "Really. I won't do it again. And I'll learn to handle the phones better and do the filing and everything. Please," she pleaded. "I really need this job."

Lani didn't even hesitate. Kim was young and inexperienced and having Al Duffy or anyone else growling at you, even over the phone, was enough to make anyone turn tail and run. And it was partly her own fault, anyway, Lani thought. If she had taken the time to train Kim better in the first place, this wouldn't have happened. She smiled reassuringly. "Okay, you're back on the payroll."

Kim let out and audible sigh. "Thank you. You won't regret it, Lani. I promise," she said, still not quite meeting her boss's eyes. "Now, what can I do?"

"You can go ahead and finish the filing you've started there." Lani pulled out the captain's chair behind the desk. "I'm going to work on the books."

"Filing?"

Lani nodded toward the file cabinet.

"Oh, the filing. Sure."

Lani settled herself behind the desk, pulled a notepad toward her and pushed the rewind button on the message machine. There was another message from Rich. "Heading over to Haliewa to check out the curls," she thought he'd said, or maybe it was "girls." With Rich it could be either one. He was due for a little relaxation, of course, and he always took a few days off after coming back from a long cruise but she wished, just this once, that he'd stuck around. She could have used his help.

But that was Rich, she thought, shrugging. His wahines, wine and song came before anything else. She shook her head, a trace of an indulgent smile on her lips, her pencil poised for the rest of the messages.

"Lani?" said Kim from behind her as she was erasing and resetting the tape.

"Just a minute." The tape whirred to a stop and she looked up. "What is it, Kim?"

"I'm not sure where this goes," the teenager said, holding up an invoice with a red stamp saying Paid across it.

"Let me see." Lani held out her hand for the paper. It was a bill from a local provisioning company. Nothing complicated about it. "Under 'F' for Food Locker," she said, giving it back to Kim. "We file everything by company name, remember?"

"Okay."

Five minutes later there was another request. "Lani, does this one go in the client files or under vendors?"

"Is it something we paid, or something someone paid us?" she asked, without looking up.

"Both."

"Both?" Lani put down her pencil and got up. Kim handed her the creased paper. It was a statement from a vendor who had been overpaid. Money had been refunded. "It's from a vendor. That's someone we buy something from," she explained. "It gets filed under the first letter of the name of the company."

"Under 'D,' then, for Donnelly Boat Yard?"

"Yes, that's right." Lani nodded approvingly. She handed Kim another invoice. "Where would you put this one?"

They continued on for another thirty minutes, Kim slowly gaining confidence, until the "To File" folder was empty.

"You can clean the storage room," Lani said, then. "A thorough cleaning, okay, not just a hit-and-miss."

"Sure thing." Kim grinned. "And Lani?" She waited until Lani had looked up. "Thanks for taking me back," she said, and disappeared into the back room.

Lani shook her head, smiling to herself. Kim might not be the brightest girl around and she seemed a bit vague and evasive at times, but she was a sweet kid. And she tried hard. She certainly seemed to be throwing herself into cleaning the storage room at any rate, Lani decided as she finished the last of the filing and turned to her desk.

She began sorting through the In and Out baskets, stacking papers to be filed or trashed. Invoices in the "To File" stack. Old sailing magazines to be trashed. Messages and notes to herself to be looked through. She read them one at a time, either marking them for further action or slipping them into a client's file or adding them to the growing pile to be trashed until she came across one from Rich written in his own hand.

It wasn't really a message at all. It looked, in fact, as if he'd absentmindedly doodled while on the phone. She read the name of the supplier, one that she'd been having some disputes with lately over billing. The words "Double order" were written under that.

Double order of what? she thought, frowning. Doubling the order would make it twice their standard order. Why would Rich be ordering double of something without discussing it with her first? When had he ordered it? Why had he—

And then she paused, crushing the pink slip of paper in her hand, suddenly remembering arguments with other suppliers over other invoices for things she hadn't remembered ordering.

Had Rich ordered those, too?

No, that was stupid, she told herself. Stupid and disloyal. There was no reason for him to have done it, for one thing. Rich didn't like "messing with all that business stuff." Too much responsibility, he said. And the last thing free-and-easy Rich wanted was any responsibility.

Still, she had been having trouble with a couple of vendors. More than a couple, really.

"God, you're getting paranoid," she said aloud, smoothing out the paper. Just because she was having a little trouble with a couple of vendors didn't mean that anyone was deliberately doing something to cause it. Certainly not Richard Billings, modern-day heir to Eros and Bacchus, the original party animal himself.

No, she decided, Rich had probably just called this supplier to check on an order or something. He did that all the time when a part for one of the boats didn't arrive when he thought it should. She'd ask him about it when he came in and they'd get it straightened out. She put the wrinkled pink slip on top of the "To Do" pile and began sorting through the rest of the papers.

"Kim?" Lani called after half an hour of industrious silence.

"What?" The teenager appeared in the doorway, mop in hand. "I'm almost finished in here, if there's anything else you want me to do."

"No, that's fine." She held up some papers. "Did you throw these invoices in the trash?"

"Invoices?" Kim's attitude was suddenly less breezy. "No, I don't touch the stuff on your desk, Lani. You told me not to."

"I'm sure you wouldn't do it intentionally, Kim, but there were three invoices in the wastebasket. I almost put them out in the garbage bin, and I—"

"I didn't touch them," Kim interrupted. "Honest, Lani. I didn't."

"Hey, don't get so upset," Lani soothed, surprised at the teenager's vehement denial. "I'm not accusing you of anything. It just seems strange, that's all, that three invoices . . . Oh, well, never mind." She turned back to her desk. "Probably I did it myself," she muttered. *Or maybe Rich had done it*, prompted a niggling little voice. But she shook her head, refusing even to consider it.

"I'm finished," Kim announced twenty minutes later. "Anything else you want me to do?"

Lani looked up from her paperwork, her expression distracted. "No, you can leave. There's just paperwork left."

Kim made a dash for the door. "See ya."

"Tomorrow after school," Lani called after her. "Three-thirty, no later," she warned, but the door had already slammed shut.

She finished checking the invoices, putting aside the ones that didn't quite tally to discuss with Rich later. Together they would go over them and see if they could figure out what the problem was.

She returned all her calls then, setting up a few day tours for next week, promising to send some brochures to a family on the mainland who were planning a future vacation to the islands, leaving messages on other people's machines when she couldn't get through. She spent another thirty minutes soothing Al Duffy, finally promising to go through the scheduling book page by page to be sure that there were no other surprises in store.

At five o'clock she stood up and stretched, easing the muscles made taut by a day spent behind a desk. Gathering up the account ledger, the month's bank statement and a stack of invoices an inch thick, she headed out to her car to be home in plenty of time for dinner.

It wouldn't do to be absent again. Her grandmother might commit hara-kiri, the ancient, honorable, and very final, Japanese way of resolving a great loss of face. Only, Lani thought, smiling to herself as she locked up the office, Sumiko would probably run the ceremonial sword through Lani's stomach instead of her own.

10

SHE NEEDN'T HAVE HURRIED home.

"Wesley called earlier," Sumiko told her granddaughter over the low basket of hibiscus that decorated the glass-topped table. "He and David will be working very late, he said, and they will 'order something in.'" The slight note of disapproval in her voice conveyed exactly what she thought of fast food.

As a result of his defection, though, they were eating informally tonight, outside on the lanai instead of inside at the low Japanese-style dining-room table. Sumiko, as casual as she ever got, was wearing a plain peach kimono. Her hair was done in a simple knot at the back of her head. Lani had opted for the comfort of a loose, floor-length Hawaiian muumuu in a vivid blend of hot pinks and purples that set off her smooth tanned skin and glossy hair to perfection.

"Did he say why they're working so late?" Lani asked, trying to appear casual as she scooped up a melon ball from the fruit salad in front of her.

Sumiko looked pleased at her interest. "The inventory is almost completed. Tonight and, perhaps, a little more tomorrow and it will be done."

Lani felt something twist inside her. When the inventory was finished, Wes would leave—for the mainland or the open sea. It didn't make any difference. He would be gone. But that's what she wanted. Wasn't it? When he was gone, so was the danger to her. But what kind of danger? she asked herself. Danger to her life? Her morals? Her business? Or her heart?

"Since Wesley will not be joining us this evening," Sumiko said as they sipped the last of their tea, "perhaps you would indulge me with a game of backgammon?"

Lani lost badly because she couldn't seem to concentrate. *Oh, Lord*, she kept thinking, *is it really my* heart *that's in danger?*

TEN O'CLOCK CAME AND WENT. Sumiko and Fomi had long since retired for the night. And Lani still sat at the kitchen table where she had moved after the backgammon game, a worn pencil in her hand, the Sail Away ledger open in front of her, trying to figure out what she was doing wrong. She couldn't seem to get the balance shown on the bank statement and the one in the ledger to agree. In fact, they were nowhere near agreeing and she was at a loss as to why.

Her father had always done the books and had never used an accountant, so it couldn't be that hard, she reasoned, tossing the pencil down in disgust. Maybe if he had, she would have had someone to turn to for advice now.

No, it wasn't his fault, she chastised herself. Her father had had no way of foreseeing his untimely death. He had quite naturally assumed that he'd have years yet to teach her the business side of Sail Away. And, to be perfectly honest, she would have resisted any effort on his part to teach her, anyway. Then and now, paperwork bored her to tears.

And it didn't help that all she could seem to think about was Wes and last night. Oh, last night.

She leaned back in her chair, closed her eyes and slowly massaged her temples with the tips of her fingers. It had been a mistake, she realized. Something that should never have happened. A one-night stand was all it was, and nothing could come of it. She didn't *want* anything to come of it. She was perfectly happy with her life just the way it was.

Or she would be when she got these damned accounts to balance.

"Hell!" she said aloud. She got up, filched a handful of cookies from the pagoda-shaped jar on the counter, poured herself a glass of milk and plopped back down in her chair. Crossing her legs Indian fashion, she tucked her skirt between her thighs and sat there, nibbling on a cookie while she stared morosely at the ledger and invoices spread out on the table in front of her.

Maybe she should ask Dave Yamazaki to help her with the accounts, she thought, and then discarded the idea. Dave was her grandmother's most faithful employee. Anything he knew, Sumiko would know. And Lani didn't want her grandmother to know how much trouble she was having with the books. It would only add fuel to her arguments against Sail Away. The only thing to do was to plow into them again and hope she came up with an answer this time. Sighing, she reached for the stubby pencil to begin work again.

"You're up late," said a voice from the doorway.

Lani jumped, brushing an invoice from the table with her sudden movement. She leaned sideways, grabbing it in midair.

"Sorry, Moonmaid, I didn't mean to scare you." Wes came around the table and pulled out the chair across from her.

"You didn't scare me," Lani denied, her eyes on the invoice she was smoothing against the table. "I was just so involved that I didn't hear you come in."

"I was being quiet," he agreed, reaching for a cookie. His eyes were on the curve of her shoulder where it met the little cap sleeve of her colorful muumuu. The bold colors were spectacular against the glow of her tanned skin. He thought about how it had looked slicked with water, about how it felt flushed with heat beneath his hands. "I thought everyone was asleep until I saw the light in here." He put the cookie down and got up. Crossing the kitchen in two long strides, he opened the refrigerator door and took out a carton of milk. "Glasses?"

"Cupboard to the left of the sink," Lani told him, watching the muscles in his broad back flex and contract against his shirt as he opened and closed the cupboard. She remembered how powerful they'd looked, just before he'd stepped into the shower, how they'd felt under her clutching fingers.

"What are you working on?" he asked as he sat back down.

"Just Sail Away's accounts," she said casually, as if she wasn't remembering that they had spent last night in each other's arms. "You're back early," she said for something to say.

"Early?" He glanced at his watch. "Late, I'd say. It's after eleven." He stretched, linking his hands above his head for a moment. "Makes for a long day."

"Did you get any dinner?" *God, what an inane conversation!* "Gran said you might order out."

"Yeah." He grimaced and bit into his cookie. "Dave brought in some take-out tempura around eight."

Lani smiled at his expression. "No good, huh?"

"Greasy," he said, and smiled back at her. There was a question in his eyes.

Lani forced herself to look away. "So." She picked up her pencil. "How's the inventory going?"

"Just fine." His eyes dropped to the pencil in her hand. She was running it back and forth between her fingers. Caressing it. "Dave's books are in excellent order and he knows exactly where every piece of stock is, so—" he paused and took a swallow of milk, still watching her play with the pencil "—there really isn't much for me to do except verify his records. I'll be done by early tomorrow afternoon."

"The inventory was a waste of time, then?" She looked up from under her lashes and caught him staring.

She dropped the pencil. They both looked away.

"Not really." He took another swallow of milk. "The whole purpose was to save face for Dave. And—" he shrugged, those broad shoulders straining against the fabric of his pale blue shirt "—checking over the books and the inventory is never really a waste."

"No," Lani agreed. "I guess not." Without the pencil, she didn't know what to do with her hands. She folded them together in her lap and stared down at them. "So, I guess that means you'll be leaving soon, then?"

"You anxious to see me go?"

Something in his voice made her look up. He was staring at her with a particularly intense look in his blue eyes, she decided. It was a look that demanded the absolute truth. "No, not really," she hedged, and looked down again.

Wes sat silently for a moment, digesting that. *No, not really.* What the hell did that mean? That she would be sorry to see him go? That she couldn't wait to see the last of him? That she didn't care either way? Damn, but he'd never been more confused by a woman's signals in his life!

She'd come to him last night. After three days of running, she'd come to him as hot and eager as a woman had ever been for him. And now she sat there, across from him, as elusive as a San Francisco fog. Her whole body said "Don't Touch" as clearly as if the words were tattooed on her forehead.

Hadn't last night meant anything to her? Anything beyond the satisfaction of a raging, unreasonable passion? He'd thought it had. He'd spent the day hoping it had, despite the warning they had given each other last night. But now?

Now, he didn't know. And, maybe, he thought, staring at the black lace lashes shielding her averted eyes, maybe it was better if he never did.

There was no sense in starting something that they couldn't finish, he told himself, ignoring the little voice that insisted that they already had. He'd be leaving in a few days, right after he'd located a boat. And she'd be staying, running her father's business. Unless he asked her to go with him.

No, that was foolish. Stupid. A man didn't ask a woman he'd only known for four days to sail away with him because he lusted after her luscious little body. Did he?

Besides, she'd made it very clear that last night wouldn't change anything. It had only been an exercise in passion. Something that they'd both be better off forgetting. It was obvious that she already had—or was trying to.

He straightened in his chair, dragging his mind away from the picture of the two of them sailing off into the sunset on the gaff-rigged schooner *Destiner* that she kept anchored in Ala Wai Harbor.

"What are you working on there?" he said then, forcing a casual note into his voice. "And don't say account books. I've had my fill of account books today."

"Well, they are account books," she said, equally casual. "And I haven't finished with them yet, so you'll just have to take yourself out of here if you don't want to see them."

"Giving you trouble, are they?"

Lani shrugged and tilted her head slightly, causing her gleaming hair to slide over her cheek. She brushed it back impatiently. "Pa used to do them," she found herself confiding. "It's only been five months since his heart attack." She stopped, feeling the sudden tears well up. She blinked, holding them back. Her hands clasped each other tightly on the tabletop. "I'm sorry, Wes. I thought I was over this," she muttered, embarrassed. He'd be bound to misunderstand if she cried now, thinking that it had something to do with last night.

But he didn't. "Don't be sorry," he said gently, forcibly stopping himself from reaching across the table to brush at the tears that hovered on her lower lashes. "It's not easy to come to terms with the loss of someone you love. I know, I lost both my parents in a car accident."

"Oh, Wes, I'm sorry."

"There's no need." Giving in to the need to touch her, he reached out and covered her clasped hands with one of his. "It happened a long time ago when I was still in my teens."

"And your Uncle Gerard took you in and brought you up?"

"Yes," he agreed, nodding. "And we've been baching it together ever since." He squeezed her hands, once, and let go. "Now," he said, reaching out and twirling her account book around to face him, "let's see what your problem is."

Lani opened her mouth to protest but he was already flipping back and forth through the pages, his long fingers competently shuffling through her checkbook ledger. After ten or fifteen minutes he looked up.

"Here's one problem, Moonmaid." He pointed to a figure. "Right here. You've transposed the numbers. It should be $2,100.00, not $1,200.00. And you didn't subtract the check charge."

"Where?"

"Right here. Twelve fifty-six."

"No, not that." She unfolded her legs from under her and rose, coming around the table to read over his shoulder. "The transposed figures. Where?"

"Here. And here, too, I think," he added, as her eyes followed his finger down the page. "It's been erased so many times that it's hard to tell."

"Damn," she muttered. "And I tried to be so careful, too." Wes turned his head to look up at her. "I seem to do that a lot." She gulped, suddenly realizing how close they were. Her hand was resting on one of his broad shoulders as if it belonged there. Her breast was brushing lightly against the other as she leaned over him. Her cheek was inches from his lips as he turned toward her to listen. "Transposing figures, I mean," she finished, straightening. She moved back to her side of the table and sat down.

His eyes followed her for a moment—smoldering, longing, vaguely hurt—and then he looked down at the ledger again. He figured for twenty minutes longer, occasionally flipping back through the pages to check a figure or thumbing through the check stubs to verify an entry.

Lani fidgeted in her chair, fighting the insane urge to get up and go to him. She wanted to smooth the springy, sunstreaked curls that caressed the tops of his ears. She wanted to trace the little scar on his jaw with the tip of her tongue. She wanted to touch the crisp, golden hairs that peeked out of the open wedge of his shirt. She wanted him to look up at her with that predatory gleam in his blue eyes. She wanted too much.

"There, that should do it." He whirled the open book around on the table so that it faced her again.

Lani hastily lowered her eyes to it. "That was fast," she murmured, feeling foolish and on fire. "Makes me feel so dumb."

"No reason you should. I've had years more practice, remember. And I like doing it." *But I'd like laying you down on this table even more. I'd like to watch you explode like you did last night.* "Just watch those transpositions," he managed, tying to ignore the images his thoughts had conjured up. He knew he could do it. Because she felt what he felt. Almost. But for some reason "almost" wasn't good enough. He wanted everything.

"Yes, I'll watch them," Lani said.

"And I'd suggest that you ask Dave to give you a hand until you get the hang of it."

She shook her head slightly.

"Don't trust him, either, huh?" Wes said dryly.

"Oh, no, it's not a matter of trusting him. I trust him."

"But not with your business."

"Well, no, not exactly," she faltered, wondering why it seemed as if they were discussing her trust of something—or someone else entirely. "Dave's first loyalty is to my grandmother," she said. "And it would be unfair of me to put a strain on that loyalty by asking him to help me with something that she disapproves of. Besides," her chin lifted slightly, "I can do it."

Wes pushed his chair back and stood up, his eyes on that delectable, bite-size chin thrust out at him. "Suit yourself," he said.

"I intend to."

He stood there, staring down at her as if waiting for something more.

"Well, uh, thank you." She touched the ledger with one hand as his eyebrow rose questioningly. "For your help with the books."

He nodded and picked up his empty glass, crossing the room to rinse it in the sink. "You're welcome," he said, pulling a dish towel off its peg to dry it.

"Wes?" she said to his back.

He continued drying the glass. "What?"

"You won't tell my grandmother, will you?"

He returned the glass to the cupboard and turned around to face her. His hips were braced against the counter, his arms folded across his chest. "About last night, you mean?"

Lani fingered the edges of the ledger, ruffling them with her thumb. "No, not about last night," she said, flushing. "I mean about the accounts. If Gran knew I was having trouble with them, she'd just use it as another argument against my running Sail Away."

"No, I won't tell her—if you'll do something for me," he added, before he could tell himself not to.

"What?"

"Invite me to go sailing like you promised."

It was a bad idea. A very bad idea. Him and her, alone, on a boat in the middle of the ocean, sailing into secluded coves.... A terrible idea. "Okay," she heard herself say. "When?"

"Tomorrow afternoon, about two?" he suggested, keeping his careless pose against the counter with sheer will. All he wanted to do was lunge forward and haul her up out of that chair and into his arms. "I should be finished at Walsh Imports by then."

"Okay," Lani said again, wondering if she'd lost what was left of her mind. "Two sounds fine. I'll have Fomi pack us a picnic—or I'll pick up something at a deli. You can meet me at the Sail Away office when you're finished at Walsh Imports."

"Till tomorrow then." He pushed himself away from the counter and moved toward the door to the lanai.

Lani twisted around in her chair to keep him in sight. There was one more small thing. "Wes?"

He stopped. "What?"

"This will be strictly platonic, won't it?"

He looked at her inquiringly.

"Tomorrow," she said. "I want you to promise that it will be strictly platonic. That we treat each other as if last night never happened."

"Do you think we can?"

Lani nodded, not trusting herself to speak.

"All right," he said. "Last night never happened."

Lani stared after him for a long moment after he had disappeared into the night, a half-wistful, half-panicked expression on her face, wondering if she should call him back and tell him that they weren't going sailing after all. It would be the smart thing to do, she knew, but . . .

She sighed and began gathering up the papers and invoices that littered the kitchen table. Some brief, penciled-in notes that Wes had made in the ledger caused her to pause and look more closely at what he had done. There were bold slashes through a couple of items with the correct amount penciled in beside them. Question marks had been placed beside a few others.

"That's odd." She didn't remember doing *that* much erasing.

The words "Paid twice?" caught her eye and she bent to study the entry. It was a bill from the shipyard at Haliewa for some bottom work done on one of the fishing boats. And further down, dated only a few days later was the same amount to the same shipyard. But was it for the same boat? There were seven boats in Sail Away's fishing fleet—the Seven Sins her father had christened them—so it could have been two different boats. But Al made it a point never to have more than one out of operation at a time. And hadn't he said something the other day, when they'd had that talk about the scheduling mix-up, about the *Gluttony* being in dry dock? Three boats in one month?

She shook her head in confusion and denial. Al would never have three boats out of commission at once. The shipyard must be double-billing them, she decided, firmly pushing aside the disloyal thought that Rich might have something to do with it since he had access to the account books. Besides, she reminded herself, Al always initialed his invoices before he sent them to her for payment, so she'd know they were okay to pay. He'd done the same thing when her father was alive.

No, the shipyard *must* be double-billing them, perhaps thinking that they could take advantage of her now that her father was no longer around. It wasn't beyond the realm of possibility. In fact, she thought, it was very possible. It didn't take much for her to imagine that a shipyard owner over at Haliewa was double-billing them, thinking that no one would notice.

But she had. And, first thing tomorrow, before anything else, she would call Al and alert him to what the shipyard was up to.

With a small, satisfied sigh, she flicked off the light switch. Hugging her paperwork to her breast, she headed slowly out the door and across the lanai and garden to her room, never realizing that Wes was sitting in the shadows, a cheroot at his lips, watching her with longing and desire—and determination—in his blue eyes.

AL WAS UNAVAILABLE when Lani called him the next morning so she was forced to leave a message, merely asking him to get in touch with her as soon as possible. Her next order of business, after pulling up the bamboo shade on the plate-glass window, was to call Rich's "emergency only" number and get him to come in and take over her afternoon cruise today. She also wanted to talk to him about the discarded invoices and the ledger—to know, for sure, that he didn't have anything to do with them.

"Rich Billings, please," Lani said to the woman who answered the phone on the seventh ring. There was some mumbling and a giggle, and then Rich came on the line.

"Yeah?" he slurred, still groggy with sleep. "Who's this?"

"It's me. Lani."

"Oh, hiya, Squirt." He yawned into the phone. "What's up?"

"I need you to come in this afternoon, Rich. I have an emergency." An afternoon sail with Wes certainly qualified as such, she defended herself mentally. "And I need to talk to you, too, about some, uh—" she forced herself to sound neither accusing or suspicious "—some invoices that don't quite add up."

"Invoices?" She sensed a sudden alertness in his tone, as if he were really listening now. "What invoices?"

"Just some invoices I came across that don't quite—"

The front door of the office opened, and a young couple came in. Lani motioned them to sit down, indicating that she'd be off the phone in a minute.

"Listen, Rich, someone just came in."

"What invoices, Lani?"

"We'll talk about it this afternoon, okay? You'll be here, won't you? Around one o'clock?" She wasn't meeting Wes until two.

"Yeah, Squirt. I'll be there. You can count on it."

"Thanks, Rich," she said, and hung up the phone.

The young couple turned out to be potential customers, interested in a short cruise if it could be arranged to happen before their honeymoon was over. By the time they had agreed on a date and time and price, Lani's first charter of the day had arrived.

The two couples vacationing together, and a third twosome they had met on the beach, turned out to be no trouble at all. One couple were good sailors and Lani was quite happy to let them handle the *Wave Dancer* after she had navigated the harbor channel.

It was one o'clock when they returned to Ala Wai Harbor, one-fifteen by the time they were docked, one-thirty by the time Lani came skidding into the Sail Away office. Rich was waiting for her.

So was Wes.

Rich grinned at her from the captain's chair. He had his feet propped up on the desk, his arms folded behind his shaggy blond head. "Some emergency, Squirt," he said, tilting his head toward Wes.

Lani tried to wither him with a glare. "You're early," she said to Wes.

"Not by much," he countered. He had waited as long as he could before leaving Walsh Imports. He and Dave had been finished by twelve-thirty but arriving then, he knew, would have been pushing it. "We said 'around two' and it's—" he gestured toward the ship's clock on the wall "—around two," he said, challenge in his voice.

Lani nibbled at her lower lip. "I haven't had a chance to get to the deli yet." And she wouldn't be able to discuss those invoices with Rich, either.

"No problem." He pointed at the picnic basket in the chair next to him. It had a blue windbreaker folded over the top of it. "I had Fomi pack us a lunch before I left this morning. It'll be better than deli food."

Lani couldn't argue that. "I had a few things I wanted to do before we left," she said.

"Go ahead," Wes invited. "I'll wait."

Which, she thought, was exactly the problem. She wasn't about to discuss the invoice problem in front of him. It might give him the wrong idea about Rich. And she wasn't about to tell him to get lost for the next thirty minutes, either. That would give him an even worse idea, besides being unspeakably rude.

"We can talk later, Squirt," Rich said. "You go on."

Lani hesitated.

"Go ahead. I'll hold down the fort here."

"You're sure?"

"I'm sure." He waved toward the door with both hands, like a prince dismissing his courtiers. "Go."

Wes stood up, grabbing the picnic basket handles as he rose. "You heard the man," he said, reaching for Lani's hand. "Let's get going." He pretended to drag her toward the door. Laughing, half willing, half not, Lani let him.

"We'll have to stop at the harbor office for a bag of ice for the cooler," she said when they were outside. "That is—" she cast a sidelong glance at the picnic basket dangling from his other hand "—unless you had Fomi pack that, too."

"Nope." He dropped her hand, looping his arm around her shoulders instead. "Lead on," he instructed, breathing in the faint, sweet, sandalwood-and-roses fragrance of her hair as they headed toward the docks.

It was exactly the same gesture that Rich had made less than a week ago, Lani told herself. The same, but different, too. Where Rich's arm had been impersonal and brotherly, Wes's was somehow intimate. Her shoulder seemed to fit just that much more snugly under the curve of his, and his hand was caressing her bare upper arm almost absently, as if his fingers enjoyed the softness of her skin, independent of his mind.

"Which boat are we taking?"

"*Destiner*," Lani said a little breathlessly. Tiny fusions of heat were dancing up her arm. She wondered if she'd be this aware of him if they hadn't made love.

"The blue and white schooner?"

Lani nodded. "One of the smaller boats would be fine, I know, but I don't get much chance to sail *Destiner* these days. She's usually out on long cruises."

Wes nodded understandingly. "She's a beautiful boat," he agreed, dropping his arm as they reached the ice machine.

The harbor master came out of the office to take their money. "Hey, Lani," he said, by way of greeting.

"Hey, Chico. How's it going?"

"Can't complain. You takin' him out for a test sail?" he said, indicating Wes with a jerk of his head.

"Test sail?" Lani repeated.

"Yeah, you know, like a test drive before somebody buys a car?"

"Buys a . . . ?" Lani shook her head. "I'm not selling anything, Chico."

"No?" The harbor master scratched his head. "Well, I didn't think so but I kinda wondered."

"How much?" Wes said then, pulling his wallet out of a back pocket. "For the ice?"

"That'll be two-fifty."

"Wondered what, Chico?" Lani asked, her eyes sliding sidelong to Wes.

"Well, after seeing this guy here nosin' around the *Destiner*, I wondered if you might'a changed your mind. I mean, what with your grandma bein' against you runnin' Sail Away and all. I thought maybe—"

"Come on, Lani," Wes said, reaching to put his arm around her shoulders again. "We'd better be going."

Lani shook him off. "Well, you thought wrong," she said firmly. "Both of you," she added, darting a quick, killing glance at Wes. "I haven't got any intention of selling *Destiner*, or any of my other boats, either."

"Well, no need to bite my head off," the harbor master objected, shaking his head as he turned to go back into his office.

Wes reached for Lani's hand.

"Why were you 'nosin'' around *Destiner*?" she asked, digging in her heels.

"I wasn't 'nosin'' around anything. I just walked by and took a look that's all. I like sailboats, remember?"

"And you're looking to buy one, too," she accused.

"But not yours," he said, exasperated. "I was just curious, okay?"

Her eyes narrowed suspiciously. "Then why the guilty act when Chico mentioned it?"

"Because I knew you'd react exactly this way, that's why. And I didn't want to spoil our afternoon."

Lani was silent, considering him from under her lashes. That could be the exact truth. Or he could know that Sumiko carried the pink slip on *Destiner* and was free to sell it anytime she wanted. Not that she would, but damn, she hated being so suspicious of everyone and everything. But there was so much to be suspicious of right now.

"Is our afternoon spoiled, Lani?" Wes asked.

"No." She wanted this afternoon with him and, dammit, she was going to take it! She'd worry about his motives tomorrow. "Let's go."

Breathing a sigh of relief, Wes put his arm around her shoulders again and turned her toward *Destiner*'s slip.

They had a perfect day for their sail. The sky was the clear, cloudless blue of fairy tales. The sea was a changing ribbon of azure and turquoise and sea-foam green as it slid past the gleaming white hull. The winds were favorable and refreshingly brisk, billowing *Destiner*'s sails so that she looked like a proud dowager queen with her head erect and her chest puffed out.

The course Lani had plotted would take them past Diamond Head and Koko Head, around the southeast tip of Oahu, past Wiamanalo Bay to a final destination just below Makapu Peninsula where Lani knew of a small, sheltered cove with a beautiful slice of beach, accessible only by boat, exactly as promised.

"Look! Oh, Wes, look," she shouted excitedly, not long after Koko Head had slid past their port side. She clutched his arm with one hand, pointing back over the stern with the other. Three porpoises were surfing in *Destiner*'s wake, their sleek, gun-metal gray bodies glistening in the sunlight. They seemed almost to be laughing with their button eyes and their mouths curved up in a perpetual grin.

"They look so happy," Lani said, her black eyes sparkling as she watched them. "It's a good omen, you know, to have them trail your boat," she informed Wes, still clutching his arm. "It means we'll have a perfectly lovely day."

"According to whom, I wonder?"

"Hmm-mm? What did you say?" she murmured, turning slightly to look at him.

"I was wondering if a perfect day would be the same for both of us."

Lani frowned at him, not understanding. He leered comically, wriggling his eyebrows at her like a vaudeville comedian, and she caught his meaning. She dropped his arm and turned her back on him, feigning an interest in the porpoises that she was suddenly far from feeling.

"Oh, they're leaving," she said as all three dived in unison. "We don't go fast enough for them and they're bored, I guess." She kept her eyes glued to the spot where they had disappeared, hoping the playful animals would reappear. "Do you get porpoises in San Francisco Bay?" she asked after a minute, turning to resettle herself a safe distance away from Wes.

"Not in the bay. At least, the *Whodunit* never has."

They rounded the tip of Oahu, coming on the windward side of the island, and Wes gave the wheel to Lani while he went forward to adjust the sails. Lani accepted it casually, lazily draping one wrist between the spokes as she kept *Destiner* on course.

Wes was an excellent sailor, even better than she had realized the other night on the *Wave Dancer*. He moved easily on the rolling deck with a certain economy of movement, a sureness that made her feel secure about leaving the bulk of the sailing to him this time out. There were very few people she trusted to pilot one of her boats and it surprised her that she could so easily give the privilege to him.

What didn't surprise her was that he would accept that privilege. Not in an imperious or overbearing way, which she might have expected—and objected to—but in an easy, casual way. Try as she might, she couldn't seem to garner up any objections. Had it been anyone else, even Rich, she would have been on her feet long before now, hotly defending her rights as captain. With mild alarm she realized that, since it was Wes, she didn't even resent it.

All the more reason, she argued with herself, to make some objection or lodge a complaint. But it wasn't hurting anything for Wes to play captain, was it? Besides, it was a glorious day and she didn't feel like making an issue out of nothing.

With a small sigh, half-resigned and, strangely, half-content, she gave up the wheel when Wes came back to the cockpit, and went below to get them a couple of beers. Her ban on drinking—in moderation, anyway—didn't extend to the times when there were no paying customers on board.

"Bring up the piloting chart for this cove we're heading for, too," Wes called after her.

"We don't need the charts," she said when she came topside again. She handed him an opened beer. "I can get in and out of that cove blindfolded." She gestured at him with her can of beer. "Move over," she ordered.

Wes scooted out of her way.

"The channel's pretty narrow but more than deep enough for *Destiner*. She only draws eight feet," Lani said, referring to the portion of the boat below the waterline. "You can see the channel, right there." She stood up behind the wheel, her feet braced wide, and pointed. "See, where the water changes color?"

Wes squinted over her head. "Looks awfully narrow."

Lani twisted around to grin at him. "Chicken?"

"I'd trust you with my life," he affirmed immediately, surprised to realize that, behind the wheel of a boat, anyway, he would. And without a qualm.

Lani turned back to the wheel, her attention on *Destiner*'s bow as the boat nosed into the channel. A wave swelled behind them, pushing them forward.

Wes made chicken noises from behind her.

Lani's startled laugh rang out, preceding them into the cove. Together, as if they had operated as a team many times before, they made quick work of lowering the sails and setting the anchor. And then, suddenly, it was very quiet. The cove was sheltered from the rest of the world by sheer, fern-covered cliffs rising sharply from the curved sliver of white sand beach. Their lush greenery was reflected in the shallow water that ran up to the shore, turning it to a pale, cool shade of green.

It was as if they had entered an enchanted place, a paradise long forgotten by the rest of the world. No breath of wind came over the cliffs to disturb the water or rustle the fronds of the palm trees. No blaring radios, no human laughter, not even the cry of a seabird disturbed the silence. There was just the gentle lapping of the waves against the side of the boat and the quiet crash as they washed the sandy shore.

They stood silently in *Destiner*'s cockpit, both of them unwilling to intrude upon the magical quiet. Their eyes met over the boom between them. Lani looked away and then, unable to help herself, she brought her eyes back to his. Holding her gaze, Wes leaned over the boom very slowly, giving her time to move away if she wanted to. But Lani stood mesmerized.

His mouth touched hers softly, tentatively—it was more of a question than a kiss—and then he drew back slightly and looked into her eyes, giving her another chance to move away. When she didn't, his hands came over the boom, reaching to cup her shoulders, gently pulling her closer, and his mouth came down on hers again, more firmly this time.

Lani's calm was shattered in an instant, replaced by urgent need. She felt herself begin to melt toward him—felt a wild surging in her blood that made her yearn to wrap her arms around him and beg for more. She almost did, but the boom barred her way, stopping her just in time. She wrenched away instead, moving as far away from him as the confines of the cockpit would allow.

"We'd better get the gear to shore if we're going to have a picnic," she said shakily. Then she hurried below and began haphazardly opening cabinets and storage lockers, pulling out snorkeling gear and beach towels.

"I promised you that this was going to be a platonic outing," Wes said from the hatchway. "I meant it."

Lani turned around to face him, a beach towel clutched in both hands. "And that kiss was your idea of platonic?"

"A thank-you kiss," he said, coming down the three steps into the cabin. "To show my appreciation for this beautiful place you've brought me to."

Lani's eyes narrowed.

"All right. Temporary insanity, then." He smiled cajolingly. "It won't happen again. If you're sure that's the way you want it." He stood in front of her, so close that she had to tilt her chin to meet his eyes. "Is that the way you want it, Lani?"

"Yes." She took a careful step back and felt the galley table come up against her thighs. "That's the way I want it," she lied.

Wes heaved an exaggerated sigh. "All right. A truce, then." He offered his hand. "I'll behave if you will."

"If *I* will?" she began indignantly. "I didn't . . ." Her voice trailed off as she realized he was deliberately teasing her. "Truce," she said grudgingly, and held out her hand.

He held it just a moment too long.

"Wes." The word was a warning—and a plea.

He dropped her hand. "I'll go get the raft ready."

Lani stood where she was for a moment and stared after him with something like panic on her face. She could abandon herself to this man, she realized. Not just physically but every other way, as well. Without a sliver of caution or good sense, heedless of all the solid, viable reasons not to, she could topple—Lord, maybe she already *had* toppled—into love with him.

"Why on earth did I ever agree to this picnic?" she whispered. But there was no answer. Squaring her shoulders, she finished gathering together the needed supplies. She brought the ice chest topside and then the picnic basket, silently handing them over the side to Wes to be placed in the rubber raft and taken to the beach.

He had already removed his outer garments and was moving around the boat clad only in a paid of well-worn, faded navy swim trunks. Cut like jogging shorts, they clung to his lean hips, revealing his firm, flat stomach with the golden whorl of crinkly hair that curled around his navel, and the long, hard-muscled length of his hair-dusted legs. His shoulders and arms were flexing and contracting as he lowered the supplies into the raft, and he was almost as tanned as she was.

She couldn't help but stare at him. And remember. Those lean hips had thrust against hers in the night. That flat stomach had touched hers. Those legs had entwined with hers. Those strong arms had held her. Deliberately she turned her head and went below before she gave in to temptation and jumped on him.

Definitely not a good idea, she thought again as she slowly stepped out of her clothes. The swimsuit beneath was one of her favorites—not the briefest she owned but not the most concealing, either. To Lani, though, it suddenly seemed totally inadequate, as if acres of her bare, tanned flesh were exposed. *Not that he hasn't seen it all, anyway,* she reminded herself as she bundled the beach towels under her arm and went topside. A long, low wolf whistle greeted her as she appeared in the open hatchway.

"Don't overdo it," she said sharply, embarrassed. "There's not that much to rave about."

Wes grinned up at her, his head and shoulders the only thing visible over the side of the boat as he stood balanced in the raft. "I'll concede that your—ah, charms aren't all that abundant," he said, deliberately letting his eyes rove up and down her body, "but what's there is choice." He laughed outright at her half-outraged, half-pleased expression. "Come on, give me those," he said, reaching up for the towels she carried.

Lani dropped them into his arms and then sat down on the desk with her legs dangling over the side. Pulling on a pair of swim fins, she slipped into the water. Wes untied the lines securing the raft to *Destiner*, and dived into the water after her. Surfacing beside her, he handed her a line and together they towed the raft to shore. They pulled it onto the beach, well clear of the surf, making sure that the picnic basket and cooler were shaded beneath the fringe of palm trees that skirted the sand.

They spent the next few hours snorkeling in the clear, fish-filled waters of the cove. Lani had been diving here many times but she never ceased to marvel at the beautiful and varied undersea life that flourished in the warm water of the Hawaiian islands.

She could identify most of the jewel-colored fish by name, pointing them out to Wes as they darted among the clusters of protective coral. Several of the larger varieties were unimpressed by the human visitors and stood their ground, surveying the intruders with one fishy eye. Wes and Lani would surface, then, laughing, and she'd begin to relax, thinking that they would be able to share a careless, friendly day, after all. And then a wave would unbalance them and Wes would reach out to steady her, his big hands on her naked waist. Or, heads close together, studying a shell or a strangely colored starfish, their eyes would meet and cling before skittering away, and Lani would become tinglingly aware of him all over again.

Wes made no move to kiss her, although it was killing him not to, and his hands, when he reached out to steady her or tapped her shoulder to call attention to yet another species of marine life, were as impersonal as he could make them, but he was as keenly aware of her as she was of him.

They both became hungry at the same time, racing back to shore to fall upon the food like greedy children. Fomi, as usual, had packed a feast—chilled cherry soup in a thermos, cold roast chicken, flavored with lemons and sesame seeds, a light pasta salad with bits of roasted red peppers and sun-dried tomatoes, and pineapple spears and thick slices of rich coconut cake for dessert. They devoured it all, washing it down with a bottle of chilled white wine.

"I don't know about you," Lani said, daintily licking her fingers, "but I'm stuffed." She yawned like a sleepy child. "Tired, too," she added, glancing up at the position of the sun. "I think I'll take a little nap before we head back. Okay with you?" she asked over her shoulder, busily brushing sand off her beach towel.

"Fine," Wes said, a tiny flame growing in his eyes as he watched her settle herself. The two strips of material that she called a bikini had been tormenting him all afternoon, the bright turquoise and lavender material revealing vast expanses of her smooth, taut, honey-gold skin, while just barely covering what he wanted to see most. "I think I'll join you," he said, stretching out and turning over on his stomach to hide his body's uncontrollable response to her.

Knowing he was watching from beneath his arm, she stretched lazily, wanting, with some part of her, for him to renege on their agreement of a platonic afternoon and make the first move. But he didn't. She heard his sharp intake of breath and what sounded like a mumbled curse and then silence. She sighed raggedly, both relieved and disappointed. Then, gradually, lulled by the rhythmic breaking of the waves against the sand, warmed by the sun, pleasantly worn out by the sailing and the swimming and the emotions that buffeted her, she fell asleep.

Minutes, perhaps hours later, she woke to shadows and a gentle tropical rain. It fell warmly on her face, rousing her to wakefulness. She opened her eyes, expecting to see the gray of gathering rain clouds. But it was Wes obscuring the sun and the rain fell from his dripping hair and his bronzed shoulders as he knelt over her, a supporting arm on either side of her body. "Time to wake up, Moonmaid," he said, shaking his head playfully so that more rain fell.

Lani giggled softly in answer, brushing away the drops of water with the back of her hand, not yet awake enough to be alarmed by his nearness—or her reaction to it.

"You're very beautiful when you sleep," he said.

Lani could feel her heartbeats quicken, beating in time to the pulse that had begun throbbing in her throat. She knew it was dangerous, like playing with fire, but she didn't care. "Am I?" she said softly, inviting further compliments.

He nodded solemnly. "You are," he assured her, careful not to touch her in any way. "You're even more beautiful awake, though, because I can see your eyes when you're awake." His voice had gone all husky and deep. "And your eyes are the most beautiful thing about you. So alive and expressive."

Lani's lashes fluttered once and then her eyes opened and she reached up, pulling him down to her.

There was nothing tentative in this kiss. His mouth moved over hers surely, expertly, demanding a response. Lani gave it to him. Her lips parted on a soft breath of sound, accepting his seeking tongue. Her arms tightened around his neck, pulling until the full weight of his chest rested against her breasts. Her fingers slid into the sun-kissed curls at his nape.

Wes made a low sound deep in his throat and rolled to his side, wrapping his arms around her. They lay face-to-face, belly to belly, thigh to thigh, kissing madly, wildly, only the fabric of their swimsuits between their yearning bodies. Wes ran his big, warm hand over her back, and the inward slope of her waist, coming to rest on a sweetly rounded hip as he buried his face in the curve of her neck. He had to slow down, he realized. Or stop. She'd said she wanted a platonic afternoon. And, dammit, he had promised.

But Lani tightened her arms around his neck as if fearing he might move away. Her lips were pressed against his chest, blindly seeking his flat, small nipples.

"Oh, Lord, Lani," he groaned. "I'm only human."

Her only answer was to flick one of his nipples with her tongue.

He gave another low groan and began kissing her again—her forehead and her nose and her rounded chin. Quick, light kisses that teased and tantalized. And then, finally, he claimed her mouth, his kiss wetter and hotter, going deeper than the one before.

Lani felt him loosen the strings of her bikini top and push it aside. His big, warm palm closed over her breast, swallowing it completely. His thumb brushed lightly back and forth over her taut, aching nipple. She moaned and arched her back, pressing her breast into his palm.

Burning, aching to taste all of her, Wes moved his head lower, scattering fiery, open-mouthed kisses down her throat and chest and the soft upper curve of her delicate breasts.

"Very choice," he growled softly, just before his mouth covered her pebbled nipple.

Lani stiffened in his arms and began to tremble uncontrollably, her small, slender body quaking. Her hands tensed on his shoulders, her fingers spread wide, halfway between pulling him closer and pushing him away.

But Wes was trembling, too, his hard muscles tight and quivering, his mind reeling, and he didn't feel the ambivalence of her response with any conscious part of his mind. Then his hand slipped down her naked belly to the fabric-covered delta of her thighs. Her response was unmistakable then, even to a man as far gone in passion as Wes was.

She cried out sharply, and her whole body arched, her legs instinctively pressing together against the seductive invasion of his hand as she suddenly remembered that she didn't want this. "No," she cried, pushing against his shoulders. "No, stop."

Wes stilled, suddenly knowing two things. He was in love with the delicate, trembling woman in his arms and he was, in all probability, going to end up ringing her lovely neck out of sheer frustration. He rolled off of her, falling back against the sand, and threw his forearm over his eyes.

Lani jackknifed to a sitting position, her bikini top clutched to her bosom. "Oh, Wes, I'm—"

"No. Don't say a word."

"But I—"

"Not one word," he warned from behind his arm. "Or I might forget that murder is against my principles."

Lani eyed him warily for a long moment. He had a right to be angry, she'd give him that. There were not very nice names for women who made a habit of doing what she'd just done. On the other hand, he'd started it by leaning over her like some bronzed god risen from the sea. So he had no right acting as if it were all her fault.

She came to her knees in a rush, her arms behind her as she struggled to untangle the knot in the strings of her bikini top.

There was a sigh from Wes. "Here." His voice held a hint of amusement and the resigned patience of a parent for a slow-witted child. "Let me help you with that." His hands touched her bare back.

Lani jumped. "I can do it," she said, jerking away.

"Don't be any more stubborn than you can help," he said, slapping at her hands. "You're making a mess of it."

Lani sat still and let him tie the strings and then, the moment he was finished, she jumped up and ran into the water. Making a diving leap through the incoming swells, she struck out furiously for *Destiner*, leaving Wes to gather up the picnic gear and follow her.

THE FURIOUS SWIM to the boat calmed her somewhat, causing her chest to heave with more than just emotion. She reached for the boarding ladder and pulled herself up onto the deck, her body dripping, her mind filled with a whirl of embarrassment and guilt and desire. She was tempted to haul anchor and leave him in the cove but she had enough good sense left to realize that it wouldn't be wise. Or fair.

So she stood on the deck and watched quietly as Wes loaded up the raft and towed it behind him to the boat, fighting the rising swells that wanted to push him back to shore. She reached over as he came alongside, grabbing the tow line as he tossed it on board.

Wes eyed her warily from the raft as she looped the line around a cleat. "You gonna make me walk the plank now?"

Lani shook her head. "I'm sorry," she mumbled. "I overreacted."

Wes cupped a hand behind his ear. "What? I didn't hear you."

"I overreacted," she said, louder. "What happened on the beach was as much my fault as yours."

"Yes, it was." He stood up with the ice chest in his hands. His legs were spread wide, his knees bent for balance. "Here." He set the ice chest on the deck. "Take this while I get the rest."

Lani continued to kneel there, staring at him.

"Lani?"

"I'm waiting for your apology," she said.

"My apology? For what?"

"For—" she waved her hand at the beach "—that."

"I thought we'd just established that it was your fault."

"Not *all* my fault." She glared back indignantly and planted her hands on her hips. "You started it and—"

"All right. It was partly my fault, too," Wes agreed. "Now, take this." He pushed the ice chest toward her.

Lani continued to glare at him.

"What do you want, woman? Blood?"

"A simple 'I'm sorry' will do."

"I'm sorry. Okay?"

"Okay," Lani said, taking the ice chest as he stooped for the rest of the equipment. But it wasn't okay. She was still seething with emotions that boiled just below the surface, struggling to get out. Silently she accepted the items he handed up to her—the picnic basket, the towels, the scuba gear, taking them all below to stow securely.

Wes was lashing the raft to the deck when she came topside. "There must be a storm brewing somewhere," he said when she came up behind him.

Lani glanced out over the water. Large swells were rolling in, breaking prematurely just beyond the mouth of the cove, hitting the coral reef with considerable force. A froth of curling white foam sent misty sprays of water spiraling into the air. The sun, hanging low in the sky, seemed to form a sparkling halo around each separate drop. It was beautiful, but Lani didn't pause to admire the sight. "The tide's coming in," she said.

"Maybe." Giving one last yank of the line to secure it, he stood and looked out toward the channel. "Whatever's causing them, we'd better get a move on before those breakers get any bigger." He shaded his eyes for a better look. "If they're not too dangerous already."

Lani bristled. *Destiner* was her boat and she'd be the one to decide whether it was too dangerous or not.

She brushed by him to the cockpit, not stopping to consider that although the channel was deep enough for *Destiner* to pass through, it was just barely wide enough, taking a sure hand, even in a calm sea to navigate her safely to the open water. Just a small miscalculation, or a breaker pushing them sideways at the wrong time, could cause damage to *Destiner*'s gleaming hull. The coral reef could make a mess of almost any boat. But Lani was confident in her ability and she wanted out of the cove—badly.

Her approach to the mouth of the cove was slow and careful, her eyes traveling between the bow of the boat to the narrow opening in the coral reef, mentally calculating the size of the breakers—their speed, their power—comparing them against the speed and grace of her vessel.

"Damn," she swore softly, bringing the boat around and heading inland.

Wes didn't say a word as she circled and came about. He bit his tongue as she aimed at the mouth of the cove again, lining up at a slightly different angle. He was sure that she'd see the futility of it before she did anything stupid.

But she didn't.

"What the hell are you doing?" he exploded, unable to keep his tongue between his teeth when she showed no sign of backing down. He grabbed the wheel, pulling hard. *Destiner* wallowed as a swell hit her broadside.

"What the hell are *you* doing?" Lani yelled at him, jumping on the excuse to vent whatever it was that was clawing at her insides.

"It's too dangerous."

"Give me the wheel," commanded Lani furiously. "I know what I'm doing."

"Like hell you do."

"I said give it to me!" She took it, jutting him aside with her hip. "I'm getting us out of here."

"Not with those breakers." His fingers closed warningly over hers on the wheel.

She snatched her hand away, appalled at the hot rush of feeling that coursed through her body at his touch. She was mad at him, dammit! "This is *my* boat," she stated through clenched teeth, "and—"

"And you can break her up on the reef if you want to." He released the wheel with a furious gesture. "Okay, if that's what you want, she's all yours—captain!"

Lani glared up at him defiantly and brought *Destiner* around again. She headed for the channel slowly, the small auxiliary engine chugging for all it was worth. She could see the calm waters beyond the reef and knew that, behind her, the cove was as little affected. It was only the channel that seethed with the ocean's power but that was enough. They were as effectively trapped as if a typhoon raged. The narrowness of the channel, the crashing breakers, the size of the boat, all conspired against her. If she had been in the *Wave Dancer* or *Sunbird*, she would have dared it. And made it, too, because neither of those boats was as wide, nor had as much keel as the boat she was piloting. But she couldn't do it with *Destiner* and be sure of coming away unscathed.

"All right, you win," she said, turning the boat away from the channel.

Wes let out his breath and then, without a word, headed to the bow to set the anchor again.

Lani watched him move away from her, amazed and grateful that not a single I-told-you-so had passed his lips. Instead he wore a curiously understanding look as he moved capably around.

Oh, hell, she thought. *Curse and rot him and his understanding and his physical beauty and his dangerous appeal!*

"Are you all right?" Wes's voice held genuine concern.

"What?" Lani looked up, confused. How long had he been watching her? "Yes, I'm fine."

"For a minute there, you looked like you were in pain."

"Did I?" she said, feigning unconcern. "I was thinking that I should call Gran."

Wes produced a creditable chuckle of amusement. "Call me if you need an ally," he said as she disappeared down the hatch.

After taking a minute to pull an oversized, thigh-length sweatshirt on over her suit, Lani raised the marine operator on *Destiner*'s radio and gave her grandmother's telephone number. Sumiko seemed surprisingly unconcerned over her granddaughter's plight, merely inquiring if they had enough food and water to last the night. Being assured that they did, she advised Lani to get a good night's sleep, saying she was confident that the two of them would "observe all of the necessary proprieties."

"You bet, Gran," Lani said aloud, hoping it was true. "We'll be as proper as two nuns in church."

She called the weather station next. The answer there was about what she expected. There was a storm brewing far out to sea with no indication that it would directly affect the islands, other than with the oversized surf. The operator wasn't familiar with her particular cove but thought that they wouldn't be trapped above a day or two, as the storm was expected to blow itself out in twenty-four to forty-eight hours.

Lani sighed off. "Forty-eight hours!" she wailed. Forty-eight long hours of trying to resist temptation.

"Problem?" Wes stuck his head through the hatch.

"Depends on how you look at it," she said wryly. "I just talked to the weather station. This storm is expected to last up to forty-eight hours."

Wes stepped down into the cabin. "Look on the bright side," he said, seating himself at the galley table. "It gives us a chance to get to know each other better."

"I know you as well as I care to."

"You don't even know my middle name," he teased, deliberately ignoring her narrowed eyes.

"Gerard."

"Right." He feigned exaggerated surprise, a hint of that appealing little-boy look in his blue eyes. "How did you know?"

"Gran told me," she admitted, trying not to smile.

"Not fair." He shook his head sadly. "Now you have to tell me yours."

"Not a chance."

"We don't leave here till you do."

"We don't leave here until tomorrow in any case."

He lunged forward suddenly, capturing her wrist across the table. "Tell," he said.

Lani twisted her wrist out of his hand. "Margaret Mae," she said promptly, not wanting to give him another reason to touch her.

He let her go, and settled back on the bench seat. "How did a one-quarter geisha doll get saddled with that?"

"Pretty awful, isn't it?" she said, absently rubbing her wrist. His hold had been gentle but she could still feel the imprint of each separate finger like a brand in the soft skin of her wrist. "Margaret is my paternal grandmother's name. Mae is after my mother. But that's not the worst of it," she found herself admitting. She rarely told her full name to anyone, it was such a Hawaiian cliché.

"There's more?"

Lani nodded. "My full name is—now don't laugh," she warned, knowing he would "—Leilani Margaret Mae MacPherson."

But he didn't even crack a smile. "Leilani. That means 'heavenly flower' in Hawaiian, doesn't it?"

"Yes," she grimaced.

"It's lovely. And it suits you."

She screwed up her mouth. "Oh, thanks a bunch."

"No, really, it does."

"Well, better than my father's first choice, I guess."

"And what was that?"

"Cherry Blossom."

He laughed this time. "Cherry Blossom!" he hooted. "What stopped him?"

"My mother. I had very red hair when I was born, according to Gran, and Pop was taken with the idea of his 'little Japanese cherry blossom.' My mother convinced him that Leilani meant flower, too."

"Cherry Blossom," Wes said again, reflectively. "It would have suited you, too."

"Suited me?" Lani scoffed. "That's ridiculous."

"You're wrong," he said positively. "When you're wearing your kimono and serving dinner so submissively, it suits you perfectly."

"I'm never submissive," she said, lifting her chin.

"No?" he said provocatively and then, seeing that icy reserve slip into place, hurriedly changed his tactics. "Speaking of dinner— Is there anything to eat on this tub?"

"Watch who you're calling a tub," Lani said, but she turned and opened a cupboard over the stove. "What would you like?"

"Do *you* cook? The women's lib— Excuse me, the feminist?"

She glanced over her shoulder. "Unless you want to?"

He shook his head, smiling lazily.

"I thought not." She lifted a hand and rummaged through the open cupboard. "We have crackers." She shook the box. "Probably stale. Instant coffee, chocolate bars, popcorn, peanut butter and jelly."

"What kind?"

"Grape and—" she pushed a jar aside "boysenberry."

"Strawberry's my favorite," he said mournfully.

"Too bad. Oh, what luck! Peppermint drops."

"You call that luck?" Wes waved away the bag she offered.

"Nothing sounds good, huh?" she said, speaking around the hard candy in her mouth. She consulted a list thumbtacked to the inside of the cupboard. "There are a few other things left over from the last cruise." She ran a finger down the neatly typed column of foodstuffs. "Assorted canned veggies, mostly green beans. Soup. Pineapple juice. A couple of cans of baked beans, chili con carne, brown bread and bacon. According to this there are even two cans of peaches left. And eggs." Skeptical of this last item, she turned and lifted the lid of a Styrofoam chest secured to the bulkhead and poked her fingers down into the bed of salt it contained. "Yep, about four or five eggs. We could have bacon and eggs," she suggested.

"How old are those eggs?"

"About five weeks, but they're still good. Really." She pulled one out to show him. "We coat them in lard, see, to seal out the air and then pack them in salt. As long as they don't get cracked, they'll last for months."

"How 'bout the chili?"

"Chicken," she accused him.

"Cluck, cluck," he agreed amiably, making her laugh as she pushed the egg back into the salt. She wiped her hands down the front of her sweatshirt. "You'll have to get up. The canned goods are stowed under the bench."

Wes slid his lean frame across the bench seat, raising the lid as he stood up, and moved to one side to allow Lani access to the food locker. But he was still disturbingly close as she bent over to pick out the right cans. She straightened quickly, as if she felt his eyes on her backside, and turned, her arms full of cans. He was right there, silently taking the cans from her to place them on a narrow counter by the gimballed stove.

The air in the tiny cabin changed suddenly, becoming charged with tension, like electrical sparks flashing dangerously between them. The atmosphere of friendly companionship vanished completely in an instant, leaving Lani standing mute and tense before him, her eyes staring fixedly at his bare, hairy chest. She was acutely, wretchedly aware of wanting only to lay her head against him and feel his strong arms close around her. She put one finger against his chest and pushed lightly. "I need room to work," she said, willing her voice not to shake.

Wes captured her hand in his, pushing her palm flat against his chest. "Now who's the coward?"

She could feel the delicious heat of his skin and the steady beat of his heart against her palm and had to fight the impulse to curl her fingers in the golden tangle of hair on his chest. "Please, Wes."

He nodded and brought her hand to his mouth. Turning it in his, he pressed a quick, hard kiss into her palm. Then he turned and left the galley before she could say another word. Lani stood where she was, pulling distractedly at the hem of her sweatshirt.

How could he do this to her? Where did he get the power to turn her bones to jelly with just a word, with just a glance from those blazing blue eyes, with just a soft, tender kiss? It wasn't fair.

She began mechanically to prepare the meal, starting the water boiling for coffee, setting the canned bacon and pineapple juice aside for breakfast, putting the peaches to cool in the ice chest, her mind all the while on the man moving around on the deck above her. Soon the chili was hot and bubbling and Lani ladled it into heavy tinware bowls, calling to Wes to ask him what he wanted to drink.

"Beer, if there's any left," he hollered, and Lani added two cans to the tray, along with the box of crackers. Stale or not, they would taste good broken up in the steaming chili.

They ate in near silence, sitting on opposite sides of the cockpit. Wes complimented her once, teasingly, on her cooking as he went below for a refill. She inquired politely, as if they were at a formal party and he were her guest, whether he'd care for dessert and coffee.

They finished their peaches and chocolate bars in the same near silence as they had consumed dinner and then Wes produced a small, thin cheroot from a zippered pocket on his windbreaker. He leaned back, stretching his long legs across the cockpit so that his feet rested on the seat next to Lani.

"Nothing like a night on the water, is there?" He gestured with the lighted cheroot. "Sweet, clean air, good food, good company." He raised his coffee mug in a kind of salute and Lani echoed his gesture, smiling faintly in acknowledgment of the compliment.

She finished her coffee slowly, needing something to do with her hands, and then fidgeted nervously when it was gone. The magical silence of the place was all around them again, intensified by the growing dusk. The light spilling from their single lantern created a soft golden glow around them, emphasizing their aloneness in the vast, fast-darkening night. Lani could no longer see the beach, just the looming black shapes of the cliffs surrounding the cove and the midnight-blue velvet sky above them lighted by a thousand glittering stars and a waning moon. She couldn't imagine a more romantic setting.

She stood up stiffly, ignoring Wes's inquiring eyebrow, and circled the deck slowly, ostensibly checking the anchor lines. Her slow circle brought her, inevitably, back to the cockpit.

"I think there's a deck of cards below deck," she said, her eyes caressing the back of his neck were the soft, tangled curls met the collar of his windbreaker. "You up for a game of gin rummy?"

"Bring 'em out," he nodded.

Lani found the cards hidden among a jumble of children's games and books stocked to keep the small fry clients happy. There was also a transistor radio. Falling happily upon this last, she tuned in a local pop station with a talky DJ. Usually she preferred what Rich termed schmaltzy music but rock was just what she needed tonight to break the romantic mood.

"Is that really necessary?" Wes asked when she appeared topside again. The radio was blaring out an old tune by Iron Butterfly.

"I like it," she lied, turning it up a little for good measure. Let either one of them get romantic with that stuff blaring in their ears, she thought with satisfaction.

Wes shrugged good-naturedly. "There's no accounting for taste, I guess," he said, taking the cards from her. "Stakes?"

"Stakes?"

He gestured with the cards. "To make it interesting."

"Oh, uh, a penny a point?"

"That's not exactly what I had in mind," he drawled, "but it'll do."

He dealt the cards and they played silently, the blare of the radio filling in the empty space around them. They were fairly evenly matched, each winning a hand and then Lani began to get painfully distracted by some of the lyrics coming from the radio. Something about spending the night together and a girl singer moaning suggestively in the background. Love songs would have been better. They, at least, wouldn't be so graphically precise.

She glanced covertly at Wes, trying to decide if he was listening, but she couldn't see his eyes. Aside from a certain tenseness around his mouth, he looked as usual, she decided, seemingly oblivious to the words coming from the radio. Lani breathed a sigh of relief and tried to ignore them herself. They played two more hands, Wes winning both easily.

"You're not concentrating," he accused her.

She jumped at the sound of his voice.

"You're letting the lyrics distract you." Someone was shouting something about wanting someone else's sex. "Some interesting ideas," he said, grinning in his wicked pirate fashion, looking even more piratic with the cheroot clamped in his teeth. "Don't you agree?"

"I wasn't paying any attention to them," she denied primly. "I just listen to the music. The beat."

"Good beat," he agreed. "Primitive. Throbbing. Like the pulse in your throat."

Lani's hand flew to her neck, her fingers covering the telltale vein. He was right, she could fell it throbbing wildly under her fingertips, corresponding to the wild beating of her heart. She forced herself to lower her hand.

"Are you going to play cards, or what?" she said coolly, leveling a challenging look at him.

We returned her look for a heartbeat, trying to read her mind, her emotions, her heart. Lani stared steadily back, daring him to take what they both so desperately wanted. Wes dropped his cards and reached out, his hand covering hers. Her cards fell to the deck on top of his, scattering like so many leaves. He stood, drawing her up with him.

"Or what," he said, tossing his cheroot overboard as he pulled her to him. They held each other for a moment, relishing the feel of their two bodies pressed together, and then he bent his head and she lifted hers. Their mouths touched and parted and touched again. Time and thought were suddenly without meaning. Shoulds and should nots disappeared into thin air. All that mattered, all that seemed real, was the two of them, alone in the dark velvet night on the wine-dark sea, their mouths sealed wetly together, their arms holding each other close.

Wes's body shuddered against her as he raised his head. "I want you, Lani. God, how I want you! But not if you're unwilling. Not if you don't want me, too."

Lani's arms tightened around him. "Does this feel as if I'm unwilling?"

"Are you sure?"

"I'm sure."

"Are you absolutely positive? You won't hate me in the morning? Or yourself? You won't regret—"

Lani stopped his words with the tip of her finger. "I'm *sure*, Wes." She was still frightened about what would come later but here, tonight, she was sure. "I want this." Her fingertip traced the curve of his lips. "I want you."

Wes's sigh came from deep within him. He bent slightly and lifted her into his arms. She clung to him, kissing his chin and cheek and the small scar on his jaw. He turned sideways, taking her through the hatchway and down the short flight of step-ladder stairs, through the galley and into the big, softly rocking bed in the main cabin of *Destiner*.

13

WES STEADIED ONE KNEE on the bed and lowered her onto the dark blue custom spread that covered it, following her down so that her slight body was pressed into the mattress. His lips covered hers, deepening immediately into a wet, open-mouthed kiss with his tongue behind it. It went on for what seemed like hours, their heads turning and shifting, their soughing breaths mingling, moisture gleaming on their lips, until finally it threatened to burn out of control if it went on a second longer.

West stopped it by lifting his head. He was going to savor her this time. He was going to love her as she deserved to be loved, with sweetness and tenderness and lots of slow, arousing touches. She had missed too much—*he* had missed too much—of the pleasure with their first furious loving.

"Lani," he murmured, disentangling himself from her clinging arms. He wanted to see her this time, too. He wanted to gaze at the velvety skin he was touching and watch her face as he entered her. "Lani, let me up so I can turn on a light."

Lani's arms fell away from his neck. "On the wall there," she murmured as he fumbled in the darkness. "At the foot of the bunk."

Soft, golden light filled the cabin, spilling from the small, lamp-shaded fixture. On his knees, Wes turned to face her. "That's much better," he said, reaching for the zipper of his windbreaker. "Much better."

Lani lay still, watching him. He shrugged out of the windbreaker, taking a small foil packet from the pocket to slip under the pillow. His swim trunks followed the windbreaker onto the floor a second later and that was it. He was as naked as he had been that day in the *furo*. But there was no water covering him now, no darkness shielding him. He was full and hard and straining eagerly toward her.

"Now you," he said, pulling Lani to a sitting position. He tugged the baggy, too-big sweatshirt over her head and then turned her, reaching for the string ties of her bikini. They were still slightly damp, the strings knotted, but he worked at them patiently until they came loose in his hands, first the one below her shoulder blades and then the one at the back of her neck. The top fell away from her body and he caught it, dropping it to the floor with the rest of their clothes.

His hands at her shoulders urged her to lie back. And then they skimmed down her torso, catching in her bikini briefs. "Lift up," he instructed softly, and drew them down her legs when she complied.

Now she was naked, too. And there was no water or darkness to shield her, either. Wes's eyes traveled over her, as arousing as a touch—a slow, tantalizing visual touch that made her skin heat and tingle. He reached out, eager to feel the beauty that he'd just devoured with his eyes. Her throat arched under his trailing fingertips, her breasts swelled, her belly quivered, her hips tensed.

She was as small and delicate as the porcelain doll he'd once compared her to but deceptively so. The long muscles in her arms and legs were strong and taut from wrestling with waves and wind. Her velvety skin, except for the lighter patches over breasts and hips, was an inviting golden brown rather than porcelain pale. The palms of her small hands were calloused from handling ropes and canvas. Wes lifted one to his lips and ran the tip of his tongue over the tiny ridge of hardened skin at the base of her fingers.

Lani gasped, her fingers curling to cup his mouth.

He lifted avid eyes to her face. "You like that?"

"Yes."

He licked her palm, slowly. "And this?"

"Yes."

"This?" he asked, dragging his tongue up the inside of her arm.

"Oh, yes."

He licked her shoulder and the delicate cords on the side of her neck. "What else do you like?" he asked, flicking her earlobe with his tongue as he stretched out beside her.

"Whatever you do to me," she said simply. It was the truth. She liked every look, every caress, every warm breath that touched her skin.

"There must be something you want," he insisted gruffly, rubbing his cheek against hers. "Some special way you like to be touched."

Lani put her hands on either side of his face and turned him to her. "You could kiss me again," she suggested.

Wes complied. Gladly. Eagerly. He touched his lips to hers, lightly at first, teasingly, until her hands were on the back of his head trying to hold him still. He used his tongue then, darting between her lips, touching it to the sensitive roof of her mouth. He used his teeth, nibbling at her lips, tugging playfully at her full lower one, closing them, ever so gently, over her rounded chin. And then he sealed his mouth to hers with a gentle suction, devouring her sweetness, until she felt limp and languid and liquid, floating on a sea of sensation, like a clear, formless jellyfish floating on the rolling waves.

His hands touched her breasts, cupping them, molding them, plumping them in his palms as if testing their slight, sweet weight. Lani moaned, pressing closer, needing more. He swept one hand down her body, skimming over the curve of her waist and hip and thigh and back up again. And then down. And up, until Lani shifted and parted her legs in silent, eloquent invitation.

Wes accepted her invitation with flattering greed, moving his hand to cover the warmth between her legs at the same time his mouth moved down to capture the breast his wandering hand had abandoned. Lani arched against him, her spine bowed, her head thrown back against the pillows, her body an open, beguiling enticement to further liberties, further pleasures.

Wes shuddered against her, feeling more tenderness, more lust, more love than he had ever felt before. He wanted her to feel the same, to know the exquisite trembling feeling that was coursing through him, to feel the power of what was happening between them. His teeth closed, ever so delicately, over the nipple in his mouth, tugging at it just as he slipped one finger into her soft, inviting wetness. They both groaned and then sighed, and Lani's hips began to move against his hand.

"Oh, that's it. That's it," he crooned, moving his finger in time to her increasingly frantic movements. She was hot against his hand. So hot. So exactly the way he wanted her. "That's it. Burn for me," he urged her. "Explode for me."

Lani lingered on the edge a few moments more, and then she gave him what he wanted. Cresting, she hung there at the peak for an endless, ecstatic, mindless moment in time. When she finally came crashing over the edge, out of breath and shaking and nearly in tears from the strength of her emotions, Wes was there to catch her. He held her for a moment, gentling her down, and then he reached under the pillow for the silver packet he had put there. But Lani had already found it.

"Let me do it," she whispered, caressing him as she completed the loving chore.

His body moved over hers, covering her as his knees slipped between her legs, pressing her thighs open to receive him. Lani closed her eyes in anticipation and ecstasy and lifted her hips.

"Look at me, Lani," he whispered, holding back at the threshold of her body. "Look at me."

Her eyes fluttered open. The look they exchanged was long and searching, rife with passion, filled with questions, brimming with need.

And then, her eyes still holding his, she wrapped her legs around his waist and pulled, locking her ankles at the small of his back. He was inside her, full and hard and wonderful, the counterpoint and complement to her slippery softness.

"Oh, God, Lani." The words were hot and hurried, rasped next to her ear as he struggled not to let it be over too soon. "You're perfect. Perfect." His voice was thick with satisfaction and intense, mind-numbing pleasure. "You're everything I need. Everything I want."

Lani moaned, telling him wordlessly of her own satisfaction and pleasure. Her legs hugged him harder and she pressed her heel into the cleft of his buttocks to urge him on.

"Sweet, sweet Leilani," he chanted, moving inside her at last. Slowly at first, and then faster and faster until her body was strung tight again, reaching, and his curved over her, driving to completion. "My sweet, beautiful, perfect Moonmaid," he crooned against her skin.

She moaned and cradled him closer, this strong, hard, exciting man who trembled like a child in her arms.

He murmured something, three quick syllables that might have been her name, just before his body tightened and burst inside her. His hips thrust forward, hard, holding her still, and a sheen of sweat broke out across his shoulder blades. But he wasn't finished yet. He reared up, back on his heels, bringing Lani with him so that they remained joined. One hand splayed on her damp back, holding her. The other slipped down between their bodies to the heat of her, finding and caressing the pulsing nub of her desire.

"Oh, Wes. Yes. Oh—" Lani crested a moment later, flung from the top of the highest wave, tumbled over and over in a wild, breathless rush to the shore.

THEY LAY TOGETHER in the aftermath, face-to-face, a pair of shipwrecked sailors, too exhausted and exhilarated by their victorious struggle to reach a safe haven to do more than hold each other. Wes cradled her body gently in both arms, pressing soft, tender kisses along her forehead and temple and the closed, quivering lids of her eyes. Lani returned his embrace, one hand tucked up between them, touching his chest, the other slowly stroking his damp back.

"I feel wonderful," he whispered. "How do you feel?"

"Wonderful, too," Lani whispered back, her lips moving against his chest as he kissed her temple. "Contented," she murmured, earning herself another soft kiss.

"No regrets?"

"Not a one." A bone-cracking yawn escaped her. "Kind of sleepy, though," she said, flattening her hand against his back as she snuggled closer. There was a soft, girlish giggle. "You wore me out."

"Sleep, then," Wes invited. He put his hand on the back of her head and tucked her under his chin. "Sleep," he whispered into her hair.

Lani sighed, burrowing into him like a kitten in familiar hands, and slept. Wes held her, listening to her soft, even breathing, feeling her small breasts pressed to his chest and her long legs tangled with his, wondering why his heart didn't burst with the feelings that swelled it. Their passion had taken him deep into a churning sea of emotion that he had only sailed the edge of before, steeping him in heat, drowning him in feeling, making him forget everything but making love to her. When he surfaced, trembling and gasping for air, everything had changed.

The woman in his arms was no longer a stranger and he was no longer *free*. A strange word to use, he thought, but true. He no longer felt free to buy himself a seaworthy boat and just sail off into the sunset now. He didn't even want to. He hadn't wanted to, he realized, ever since that morning on the lanai. What did he want instead? he asked himself. To make love to her? Well, he'd done that, he thought with satisfaction, and he planned to do it again, every chance he got. But he wanted something more.

Something like marriage.

The idea startled him and he drew back a little, staring down into Lani's sleeping face. "Marriage," he said soundlessly, testing the feel of it on his lips. It sounded right. Felt right. He cradled her closer.

Marriage.

He had never wanted it before. Never even seriously thought about it before. But now, with Lani sleeping so peacefully in his arms, his body replete with their lovemaking and his heart full, it was all he could think about.

It would probably take a while to convince her that the idea had merit. She was as independent as all hell, despite the traditional influence of her grandmother. She was stubborn, too, when she got an idea in her head or took a position on something. And she'd certainly made it clear enough that her business was her top priority. *I don't have time for a relationship right now,* she'd said that first time, letting him know that passion was all that had brought her to his bed. Well, he'd said it, too. And he'd meant it just as much as she had. Then. But not now. Because now it felt like more than passion to him.

It felt like love.

Deep, abiding love, the kind of love that was worth a few compromises, a slight shifting of priorities. She wasn't so stubborn and single-minded that she wouldn't see that eventually. If he went about it in the right way, with just the right combination of patience and passion, it shouldn't take too long to bring her around. He was a lawyer, after all. It was part of his job to make people see things his way.

Confident, his mind whirling with a thousand plans, Wes closed his eyes and fell asleep.

LANI AWAKENED the next morning to the smell of frying bacon and the sound of Wes humming off-key in the galley. She lay in the rumpled bunk, feeling languid and content and uneasy. Not sorry. Not full of regrets. Just uneasy.

What, she wondered, did you say to a man on the morning after the night before? Especially when the night before had been such a mind-blowing, soul-shattering experience and you weren't sure where the morning after was headed?

A simple "good morning" sounded a bit too casual. On the other hand, "I love you" was a tad intense the first thing in the morning. Besides, what she felt wasn't love exactly. It was close but it wasn't love. Love meant all sorts of things that she wasn't ready for at this stage of her life. Commitment. Change. Compromise. Things that he undoubtedly wasn't ready for, either, considering the fact that he intended sailing away in a few days. And yet . . .

You're everything I want, he'd said last night. *Everything I need.* But those were just pretty words uttered in the throes of passion. You couldn't hold a man to what he said at a time like that, even if you wanted to. And she didn't, did she?

No, she most emphatically didn't. Her life was complicated enough right now without adding a man to the equation. And she would tell him that, somehow, over breakfast or while they were sailing back to Ala Wai Harbor. If it was necessary to tell him anything at all. Which it probably wasn't. Neither one of them had said anything about love; they were both adults who could take passion where they found it. Almost paradise, after all, was better than no paradise at all. And, maybe, they could work something out. Some sort of no-strings-attached relationship that would leave them both free to pursue their separate goals.

"Life's a complicated bitch," she said aloud, staring at the planked ceiling above the bunk. "And I'm starving." The smell of bacon was making her mouth water. She rolled to the edge of the bunk and reached over the side, groping for her bathing suit and sweatshirt. They weren't there.

"I took your things topside and hung them over the boom to air out."

Lani angled her head to see Wes standing at the foot of the bed with a mug in one hand and a dishtowel tucked into the waistband of his blue trunks. He looked so darned gorgeous and domestic and *right* that it scared her nearly spitless. "That was thoughtful of you," she said, peering up at him through the silky curtain of her hair.

"Actually, it wasn't." He flashed his pirate's grin at her. "I just did it because I want to keep you naked and at my mercy."

Lani's heart began to beat erratically. *Naked and at his mercy.* What a lovely thought. She levered herself up onto an elbow, the sheet clutched to her breasts with one hand. "Is that for me?" She nodded at the mug.

"Mmm-hmm." He moved into the cabin and sat on the edge of the bed. "Tea, heavy on the sugar. Right?"

"Yes." She reached out and took the offered mug. "Thank you."

"You're welcome." He leaned over and kissed her bare shoulder as she sat up to sip her tea, then stayed to nuzzle.

She could smell the sea on his hair, feel the dampness as it brushed against the side of her neck. Her skin began to tingle. "Been swimming?" she asked, her hand itching to reach up and press him closer.

"Mmm-hmm," he murmured into her neck. "The water was great. If you weren't such a slug you could have gone swimming, too."

"Who says I still can't?"

Wes lifted his head and gave her a slow, smouldering look. "I do."

"Oh, really?"

"Yes, really." He reached out and took the mug from her.

"I'm not finished with that." She tried to sound indignant but only succeeded in sounding breathless.

"You can have it later. I've got other plans for you right now."

"Breakfast?"

He put his hands on her shoulders and pressed her back. "Later."

"But you've already cooked the bacon. I can smell it."

"It'll keep." He grasped a handful of the sheet.

She held on just to make him take it from her. "It'll get cold."

"We'll make BLTs."

"But we have to get back to Ala Wai, Wes." The sheet slipped from her fingers, baring her breasts. "I really should be getting back to the office to, uh . . . to . . ." The thought slipped away from her altogether as his lips touched her pebbled nipple. "Oh, well." She sighed languorously. "I can do it later."

14

"YOU GO ON HOME, WES," Lani insisted when they finally sailed into Ala Wai Harbor just after noon. "I've got work to do here. No, really," she said when he started to object. "Rich is out on *Wave Dancer*." She waved the pink slip of paper with Rich's message on it at him. "And Kim won't be in until after school. I need to stay."

And for more than just the sake of the business, she thought. She needed to be by herself for a while, away from his distracting, arousing, confusing presence. She needed, mostly, to think.

"Now, go on. Get out of here," she said when he expressed reluctance to leave her. "I've got work to do."

"You're sure?"

"Yes," she said, all but pushing him out the door. She stood just inside the threshold, watching as if to make sure he really left, letting out a breath she hadn't known she was holding when he started the engine and pulled away from the curb.

Alone at last.

And what good did it do her? she asked herself. Last night had still happened. This morning had happened. She had still slept with—no, made love with—Wes. It had been true lovemaking, no matter how much she tired to pretend it was something simpler. But she still didn't know where they were going to go from here. He might stay, of course—delaying his sail to Tahiti, or wherever it was he was headed.

But then what happened to that no-strings-attached relationship she'd been contemplating? Or dare she consider marriage?

She shook her head, unable to see herself in either scenario. She wasn't really the type for an affair. And marriage was out, even if he had proposed it, which he hadn't. Because marriage, the only kind of marriage she knew, anyway, meant commitment and compromise and, eventually, children. And end, in fact, to her dreams of running Sail Away.

Just what her grandmother had ordered.

"Hell," she said to the empty office. Her whole life was rapidly becoming as big a mess as Sail Away's books, she thought, dropping into the captain's chair behind her desk.

One of Kim's teen magazines lay open to an article on what some adolescent television star looked for in a perfect date. Lani slapped it closed and threw it into the overflowing wastebasket.

Two pieces of paper whooshed up out of the wastebasket and drifted to the floor. With a small sound of irritation, she leaned over and scooped them off the floor, intending to stuff them back into the wastebasket. Her hand checked in midmotion as a familiar letterhead caught her eye, that of the Food Locker, the provisioner she used almost exclusively to stock her cruises. The other piece of paper was an invoice from a local boat chandlery. She spread them out on her desk, all thought of her tangled love life pushed from her mind.

The letter was a dunning notice, a "second request" for payment. The invoice was for three new child-size life jackets that she'd ordered a couple of weeks ago.

What the hell? she thought, frowning. Why had they been trashed?

Then she remembered the handful of invoices she'd fished out of the wastebasket just the other day. It was just possible that she might have trashed those, but not these. The wastebasket had been empty when she'd left yesterday. Her stomach clenched painfully. Rich had been here when she left, too. Sitting right here at her desk with his feet up. Just like he had a hundred times before.

"Oh, God, no," she said aloud. Not Rich. It couldn't be Rich. But who else could it be? And then, *why?* Why would Rich want to ruin her business? Because that's what it amounted to. It just didn't make sense. And she had to make sense of it. Somehow.

Stoically, Lani upended the wastebasket on her desk and began carefully sifting through it, looking for more discarded invoices or letters. She found two, making a total of four. *For today*, she thought, wondering how many had been thrown out that she hadn't found.

She stacked them to one side of her desk and spread open the company ledger, looking for discrepancies or erasures. There were four places, maybe five, that she knew for certain she hadn't erased. She fished the checkbook out of the middle drawer of the desk to compare the figures. Five places for sure then, where the entry had been altered.

Why? What possible reason could Rich have for doing this?

But was it really Rich? Would he have warned her about making so many erasures if he had been doing them himself? Was he that diabolical? Her heart said no, and even with the evidence right in front of her, she couldn't quite make herself believe that it was wrong.

The door rattled. Lani jumped and looked up. She wasn't ready to face Rich just yet. Relief flooded through her as she saw who it was. "Oh, hi, Kim," she said dispiritedly.

"Gee, you sound grumpy. Am I late?"

Lani glanced at the clock. She'd been sitting at her desk for the better part of three hours. "No, you're not late. It's just that I am so involved with this—" she gestured at the papers on her desk "—that you startled me."

"Sorry." Kim dropped her purse onto a canvas chair and came around the desk. "What are you working on?"

"The accounts."

"Oh. Are they, um, giving you trouble?"

"You could say that," Lani admitted. She ran a hand through her hair, pushing it off her face, and turned to look up at the teenager hovering over her shoulder. "You remember those invoices that I found in the wastebasket the other day?"

"Mmm-hmm."

"Are you sure you didn't throw them away?"

Kim backed away a little. "I didn't!" she said vehemently.

Almost too vehemently, Lani thought. Was that guilt in the girl's eyes? *Really, Lani, isn't that reaching a little? Kim?* The girl could barely keep the filing straight, let alone being smart enough to finagle the books. "I'm not saying you'd do it on purpose," Lani soothed her. "It's just that—"

The front door opened again. "Hiya, ladies," Rich said cheerfully, swinging the door closed behind him so that the glass rattled in its frame. He folded his lanky self into the canvas chair in front of Lani's desk and lifted his feet to the edge. "Glad to see you made it back, Squirt." He grinned at her; it was the same sort of teasing, brother-to-sister grin as usual. "High jinks on the high seas, huh?" he said, and winked.

Lani came to a decision. She had to know. Now. "Kim, why don't you take that dead plant over there—" she gestured toward the plant on the filing cabinet "—and throw it out for me, please? And then run across the street to the deli and get us some—" She looked at Rich. "Doughnuts, okay?"

Rich nodded.

"Get us some doughnuts. You know how hungry Rich always is after a sail. Here." She dug into her tote bag and pulled out a ten dollar bill. "Get a quart of milk, too."

"Yeah, and hurry," added Rich. "I've got another tour in about fifteen minutes."

Fifteen minutes, Lani thought as Kim left. Well, fifteen minutes was enough time to find out if the man she loved like a brother was trying to ruin her business. She took a deep breath. "Rich, I've got to talk to you about the business."

"So talk," he invited. "I'm all ears."

"Well, there's been—" Oh, Lord, this was hard! "—there've been some discrepancies in the books."

Rich straightened in his chair, putting his feet on the floor. "Discrepancies?"

"Entries have been changed," she said, watching him. "There's lots of erasing so I can't tell how many for sure, not until I do some more checking."

"Are you sure you didn't do it yourself? You're not the world's best bookkeeper, you know."

"I'm not stupid, either. These entries have been deliberately changed."

Rich's mouth fell open. "Deliberately?"

"Yes." Lani nodded. "And that's not all, Rich."

He said nothing, just sat there staring at her. Was he afraid of incriminating himself if he said any more?

"There are problems with some invoices, too," she said, her voice dull with dread. "There've been some extra orders—orders that I didn't make—or we're being double-billed."

"Yeah." He leaned forward. "I know about that."

"You know?" Hope flickered. Would he admit knowledge if he was responsible?

"Yeah," he said again. "One of the vendors called to check an order one day when you were out. The order was twice our usual, and he wanted to make sure it was correct. I left a message for you on the desk about it."

"B & B Chandlery," Lani said, remembering the name penciled on the memo she had found. Relief flooded her. He'd meant for her to find the memo!

"You got the memo, then."

"Yes. But that's not all of it, Rich." She handed him the invoices. "I found these in the trash."

He took them from her, shuffled through them quickly, and then again, more slowly, thoroughly studying each one. His face, when he finally looked up at her, was as serious as she'd ever seen it. "Do you think I have something to do with this?" he said quietly.

"I wondered," she admitted, feeling wretchedly guilty and disloyal. "But I didn't really believe it," she assured him. "You wouldn't do this to me. Or anyone else."

"No," he said. "I wouldn't." He looked down at the papers clutched in his hand. "How long has this been going on, do you think?"

"I don't know, exactly. Maybe ever since Pop died?"

Rich's eyes captured hers. "Your grandmother?"

"Oh, Rich, no!" But she wasn't sure. Sumiko was dead set against her running Sail Away, but she wouldn't resort to this. Would she? Her strict sense of honor would surely forbid going this far. "I don't know," Lani said. "I just don't know." She lifted her hands helplessly. "How could she? She never comes anywhere near the office. I doubt she even knows where it is."

"She could have had someone do it for her. The office is empty often enough. And she had a key, doesn't she?"

"Yes, but—"

"And you don't lock the files or your desk, just the safe. Someone could have come in and changed the entries."

"Whoever it was fooled with the bookings, too," Lani said.

Rich nodded. "All those double-bookings and no-shows."

"I just don't think Gran would go this far," Lani said. Her eyes pleaded with Rich for another solution. "Do you?"

"She hired Wes Adams," Rich reminded her.

"To take care of an inventory problem at Walsh Imports," Lani said. "That's all."

"That's not what you thought at first."

"At first, yes, but not now. Not after he explained why he's here." It couldn't be Wes! Not after what had happened between them. He couldn't make love to her like that and then... "No, it's not Wes," she said firmly. "Wes wasn't even in the islands when all this started."

"Who, then? Who would benefit by running you out of business?"

"Our competition?" she suggested without much hope.

"Maybe," Rich agreed. "But which one? There's—"

"Got the doughnuts," Kim said, banging into the office. She placed the doughnut box and a quart of milk on the desk and dropped the change beside it.

"Thanks, Kim," Lani said distractedly. "Why don't you take a couple for yourself?" She waved at the doughnut box. "Then you can, uh...tidy up the storage room," she improvised. "Rich has managed to mess it up since you cleaned it last."

"Sure thing," Kim agreed.

Rich and Lani sat silently, staring at each other across the desk, until the girl had disappeared into the storage room.

"It can't be our competition," Lani said. "They just wouldn't have access."

"Well, then, dammit, *who*?" Rich said, his voice rising in frustration on the last word. "Who'd profit by ruining Sail Away? Think, Lani. Who?"

"I have thought but—" she shrugged "—nothing."

"Al?" he suggested, and then shook his head before she could answer.

A crash came from the back room. "Sorry," Kim called but neither of them paid any attention.

"Naw," Rich said, still mulling it over. "Al never even comes over to this side of the island. It couldn't be him."

"Then who?" Lani demanded. Who was left?

"Hell, I don't know, Lani. Maybe we should hire a private investigator or—"

There was a knock and the front door was pushed open. "Excuse me," said a feminine voice. "I'm Jill Nickols," she said when Rich and Lani looked up, "and these are my two boys. We booked a sail this afternoon."

"Oh, yeah, sure." Rich got to his feet. "I'm Rich Billings. I'll be your captain this afternoon. And this is Lani Mac Pherson, the owner of Sail Away."

"Can we go now, Mom, huh? Can we? Can we?" implored two young voices.

Jill Nickols smiled. "The boys are anxious."

"Well, then, you'd better get going." Lani rose to her feet too. "We'll talk about this later, Rich." She followed him to the door, putting her hand on his arm to hold him behind for a moment. "I'm sorry for ever even thinking that you had something to do with his mess, Rich," she said earnestly. "I love you."

"I love you, too, Squirt." He kissed her on the cheek. "Try not to worry. We'll figure it out," he promised.

Lani nodded, smiling wanly as she waved them away.

"What was that all about?" Kim asked, coming out of the back room.

"What was what all about?" Lani sat back down behind her desk.

"You and Rich seemed awful upset about something."

"Just business." Lani motioned at the chair across from her. She wasn't about to discuss Sail Away's problems with a scatterbrain like Kim but now was as good a time as any to continue with the lecture on proper office procedure. It was always possible, in fact, probable, that Kim had trashed the invoices by mistake and was too scared to admit it. "Sit down a minute, Kim."

"I'm not finished in the back yet."

"That's all right. You can finish it later. Come on." She gestured at the chair again. "Sit and we'll talk."

Nervously, Kim sat. "What about?"

"Handling invoices, for a start. I know you didn't throw—"

"I didn't throw them out on purpose, Lani!"

"Hey, I know you didn't," Lani soothed. "I just want to discuss how we can avoid mistakes like that in the future, that's all."

"I didn't do it," Kim said again.

"It doesn't matter," Lani assured her a bit testily. She wasn't pleased that Kim continued to deny it. "I'm not going to fire you for one mistake."

"I didn't do it!" The girl's words were almost a shout.

Lani stared at her, puzzled. Kim was acting as if she had something to hide. Something... Lani's eyes widened. Kim's face was flushed, her trembling hands were clutched together in her lap, and her eyes looked anywhere but at her employer.

"It was you," Lani said quietly.

"No," Kim denied. "I didn't! I just got mixed up, that's all!" She looked at Lani pleadingly. "It's very confusing. You said so yourself and—" Her voice trailed off.

"Why, Kim?"

"I told you! I didn't!"

Lani's voice cut across hers. "Yes, you did." There was utter conviction in her voice. "You threw away those invoices on purpose. And you've been altering the accounts and mixing up the bookings, too. And the other day, when I came in early, you weren't filing," she said, almost reflectively, suddenly seeing the incident in a new and disturbing light. "You were deliberately *mis*filing."

"No, I didn't! I wasn't!" Kim's eyes darted around as if looking for a way to escape. "Please! I didn't."

"Don't keep on lying to me, Kim," Lani snapped. "You deliberately falsified the schedule book. You changed figures in the cash ledger," she charged. It *had* to have been Kim—no one else had both access and opportunity. The girl's motives were still a mystery, but Lani was sure that Kim was the culprit. "That in itself is a criminal offense," she said, not really knowing if it were true since Kim was a minor. "I could have you arrested."

Kim's lips began to tremble and she tried to blink back tears.

Lani leaned forward, sensing that if she let up now, if she went around the desk to soothe the crying frightened girl, as all her kind-hearted instincts urged her to, she might never know the whole story. Deliberately she put her hand on the telephone. "Now, before I call the police and have them haul you off to jail, do you want to tell me the truth?"

At the mention of the police, Kim cracked. Her tear-filled eyes rounded in fear, and her flushed face paled and then flushed again. "I didn't want to, Lani. Honest, I didn't! B-but he said I had to. He said he'd stop my mother's support payments and...and..." She covered her face with her hands and began to cry in earnest.

Lani got up and came around the desk, unable to remain hard in the face of Kim's obvious distress. She put a comforting arm around the sobbing girl's shoulders. "All right, Kim. Calm down." She patted her. "Tell me who *he* is and I won't call the police."

Kim looked up hopefully. "I don't have to go to jail?"

"Not if you tell me who made you do this." She squeezed the girl's shoulders reassuringly and sat down on the edge of the desk. "Now, dry your eyes." She plucked a tissue out of the dispenser on the desk and handed it to Kim. "Tell me who. And why."

"I don't know why," Kim began, still tearful. "Not exactly, anyway. Honest." She wiped at her eyes and blew her nose. Lani had to restrain herself from cursing with impatience. Who? she wanted to scream. "But Uncle Al thought that you shouldn't have—"

"Uncle Al?" Lani interrupted, jumping up. *Uncle Al!* "Al Duffy is your uncle?" she asked incredulously, reaching out to grab the girl's shoulders.

Kim nodded.

"And he made you do this?"

Kim nodded again.

"Why?" Lani asked, stunned. He had no reason. No motive that she knew of. "Tell me why, Kim," she commanded.

The whole story came tumbling out then. All about how Kim's mother had married early and been widowed equally early, leaving her with three children to support. And about how her brother, Al Duffy, had contributed to that support, making the difference for the little family between poverty and getting by. And how he had threatened to cut off that support unless Kim did what he told her.

"But why?" Lani repeated, giving Kim a little shake. "Do you know why? What did he hope to gain?"

"The fishing boats, I think," Kim said. "He thought they should be his. He's worked them for the past twenty years, he said, and they should be his. And no...no woman should be running them. He said that your father promised them to him."

"Promised him!" Lani cried, unbelieving. Her hands dropped from Kim's shoulders and she sat staring blankly at the girl in front of her. "Promised him?" she said again, almost to herself. "Pop would never have reneged on a promise if he'd made one. If he'd promised Al—" She broke off and stared into space over Kim's head. There had been talk of a partnership once but nothing had ever come of it. Was that the promise Al thought had been made to him?

"Lani?"

Lani focused on Kim's face.

"What are you going to do?"

Lani stood up. "I'm going to see your uncle," she said, suddenly determined. "Right now. And you're coming with me."

"No." Kim stood, too. "I can't, Lani. He'd be so mad at me." She shook her head. "I can't."

"I'm not leaving you here to call him the minute I'm gone. I want this to be a complete surprise."

"I won't call him, Lani. I promise. Please don't make me go. Please."

"All right," Lani said, moved by the girl's plea. "You don't have to go." Short of dragging her by the hair, there was nothing Lani could do to make her go, anyway. She fixed her with a steely stare worthy of Sumiko at her most haughty. "But I'm trusting you, Kim. And I'll press charges if you're lying to me."

LANI DROVE FURIOUSLY, pressing the speed limit as close as she dared, flying along the road to Sail Away's Haliewa office on the north side of Oahu. Her mind was busy with trying to decide exactly what to say to Al when she got there. She still couldn't quite believe it. Al had been with Sail Away for so long and, if he had not exactly been a friend of her father's, he had always been a trusted employee.

For the fishing boats, Kim had said. But how would ruining Sail Away get the fishing boats for him? Double bookings put him in a bad light with the customers, just as it did her. And having Kim change the figures in the cash journal made Lani's job harder and more time-consuming, but she didn't see how that could benefit Al. And throwing away the invoices? Having the shipyards double-bill her? Why?

Her mind flittered around the edges of something but she couldn't quite grasp it. Cash, she thought, that was part of it. Lots of Sail Away's customers paid with cash, she mused. Could the muddled bookings and juggled cash journal be some sort of smoke screen to keep her from knowing exactly how much business he was really doing? A busy season, he'd said that morning when he called about the fouled-up schedules. Busier than usual? she wondered.

Fleetingly she wished that she'd taken more time to think things through, to gather evidence, before rushing off the way she had. But then, she thought, she knew enough. No matter why he had been forcing his niece to fiddle the books, the fact that he *had* was all she really needed to know.

She turned the Jeep into the marina parking lot at Haliewa and, switching off the engine, sat stiffly for a minute, gathering her courage. I wish Rich were here, she thought, her hands clutching the wheel as she sat there. Or Wes, she amended, thinking of his size and strength and the sheer force of his personality. Wes would know what to do.

But he isn't here, she told herself firmly, *and you have to handle this by yourself. And you should! It's your company. You wanted to run it. So get out and do it!* She reached for the door handle and her fingers froze in the act of opening it.

Wes *was* here!

He was coming out of the small Sail Away office with Al Duffy. They seemed to be in deep discussion, walking out toward the pier where two of the Seven Sins were anchored. Al slapped him on the back and Wes laughed, throwing his head back in a familiar gesture, looking more like a pirate than he ever had.

A sneaking, sulking cur of a pirate! Lani thought. What was he doing here? Why wasn't he at her grandmother's house? And why in hell was he talking to Al? Laughing with him as if they were old friends? Or business associates?

Then, no, she reminded herself. Wes wasn't behind her problems at Sail Away. He hadn't even been in the islands when her problems started. But he obviously knew Al, and he was here with him now, when he'd said he was going to her grandmother's.

Could she have been that wrong about someone? Could she have given her heart to a man who could make love to her one minute and conspire to ruin her business the next? Even if he was doing it on behalf of a client, it was still a despicable thing to do.

No, thought Lani again. No! Sumiko might not want her to run Sail Away but she wouldn't resort to this kind of subterfuge. And, yet, what other explanation was there? Wes was here, where he had no other reason to be.

Lani slouched down in the seat of the Jeep, almost on the floor, fighting hot tears as she waited for Wes to leave. And then, squaring her shoulders, she jumped to the ground and stormed into the Sail Away office to confront Al.

Without giving him a chance to open his mouth, she informed him in a voice cold with rage that she knew all about what he had been up to, what he had pressured Kim into doing for him. "You can consider yourself lucky. It's only because of her that I'm not pressing criminal charges."

Al sat there looking at her for a moment, his mouth hanging open, and Lani felt a faint stir of doubt—and hope. If he wasn't guilty, then neither was Wes.

But Al spoke before either feeling could grow. "We'll see who brings charges," he threatened. "I got my own lawyer."

Yes, she thought, her heart breaking. *Wes.*

"Ever hear of breach of promise?" Al sneered, thinking he had her cowed. "Me and my lawyer are gonna sue you for every penny you got."

But his reference to Wes had sealed his fate. Lani's fury flamed to the surface. The fury of a woman betrayed by her lover. "You're fired, Al," she said, very calmly and clearly.

There was ice in her black eyes. "You can pack up your personal things and leave. Now."

"And who's gonna make me?" he questioned nastily, rising menacingly from behind his desk. "You, little girl?"

Lani didn't even flinch. "Yes, me," she said. "And the police if you force me to it. What you did is called stealing, no matter how you did it. Not to mention corrupting a minor. And unless you want me to press charges, you'll leave without causing any trouble."

"I'm gonna cause trouble, all right. Real trouble. Your old man made me promises and I'm gonna see I get what's mine."

"My father never made you any promise. If he had, he'd have kept it."

"I got papers to prove it, little girl. Papers I can show in court."

"I don't believe you," Lani scoffed, throwing the words down like a gauntlet. "You're lying."

"Lying, am I?" He opened the top drawer of his desk and dug out a sheet of paper. "Here, read this."

Lani grabbed at it eagerly.

"And don't think you can tear it up. I ain't stupid enough to give you the real thing. That there's just a copy."

Lani ignored him, her eyes skimming the document in her hand. It was a rough partnership agreement, with Sail Away Tours at the top and her father's name filled in as a party of the first part. But it was undated and unsigned. The partnership that had been discussed, then, but never completed.

"This means nothing," Lani said. "Absolutely nothing."

"We'll see, little girl. We'll see."

She tossed the paper on his desk. "Yes, we'll see. But I still want you out of here today." She turned her back on him and left the office.

She walked purposely over to the harbor master's office and coolly informed him that, as owner of Sail Away Tours, she wanted her seven fishing boats off limits to Al Duffy and his crews. "I'll send someone over to padlock them tomorrow," she said. "But, until then, they're not to leave the dock."

And then she drove straight back to her office at Ala Wai Harbor and systematically called all of her suppliers to inform them that Al Duffy was no longer on Sail Away's payroll. "Please cancel any outstanding orders he may have placed," she requested in her most businesslike voice, "and send me a statement of account as of today."

Then she sat back in her captain's chair feeling drained, and sad, betrayed and triumphant, all at once, and tried to decide what she was going to say to Wes when she saw him again.

LANI SAT LISTLESSLY sipping her tea, fresh from her shower and wrapped in a short terry robe, delaying the time when she had to begin getting ready to join the group gathered in her grandmother's living room. Sumiko was having a small celebration in honor of the successfully completed inventory. Dave Yamazaki and his wife Connie were there, plus a few others from Walsh Imports, and Wes, of course.

"We have much to thank our dear Wesley for," Sumiko said when Lani finally arrived home, tired and rumpled and brimming with more emotions than she could give name to.

Her first impulse had been to confront her grandmother with what she'd found out, to demand answers for the elderly woman's actions with regard to Sail Away, to plead for some explanation that would make everything all right. But she couldn't.

Cowardly, maybe, and weak. But she couldn't, not with a houseful of guests. Her grandmother's loss of face would be devastating. Not to mention her own. Somehow she didn't care to have everyone know what her grandmother had been a party to. Oh, all for her own good, of course. Lani knew that Sumiko hadn't done it out of spite or greed or anything like that. She probably hadn't actually *done* anything, besides merely letting it be known that she would prefer that her granddaughter not be involved in her late son-in-law's business. However it had come about, Lani knew that Sumiko had only done what she thought best for her granddaughter. Lani could almost understand that and, eventually, she would forgive it.

But what she couldn't understand, or forgive, was Wes's betrayal. To have made love to her like that, all tenderness and passion, and then to turn around and stab her in the back! At the very least, she had thought Wes would understand and respect her position on Sail Away. She had even thought that he might want to share it with her.

Pride stiffened her resolve as she thought of how stupid and trusting she had been. He would never know how much he had hurt her. Never. She would get dressed and join the party as if nothing at all had happened.

Putting down her tea, she picked up her eyeliner pencil, darkening the makeup she had already applied along the lower rim of her lashes. Her eyes were expertly lined in a shade of plum so dark that it was almost black, shadowed with a soft grape, highlighted with the faintest touch of pink under the arch of her brows. Her cheekbones were dusted with a gilded rose blusher. Her lips were glossed in a coordinating shade. It was as perfect as she could make it; a glossy mask that hid the pain inside.

She rose to take her dress from the closet. A traditional strapless *pareau* made of violet silk with an artistic swirl of lavender and pink down the left side, it draped from a simulated knot between her breasts, falling in slim, graceful folds to the floor. With it she wore strappy silver sandals and long, delicate earrings of lavender jade and silver filigree.

There was a soft scratching noise at her door. "Missy Lani, please hurry," Fomi said.

"Yes, I'm coming now, Fomi," Lani said as she slid open the door.

"Oh, how pretty you look!" complimented Fomi before she turned to bustle down the hall ahead of Lani.

The party was in full swing when she arrived in the living room. If, she thought, you could ever say that one of her grandmother's sedate, elegant little gatherings ever actually "swung." All the guests were there, clustered around a table loaded with all the tasty little tidbits that Fomi would have cooked earlier and arranged so beautifully on Sumiko's lacquered trays. All of them were chatting and laughing and having a wonderful time. Wes looked up as she paused just inside the archway from the hall, his eyes widening appreciatively at the sight of her. A smile of greeting turned up his lips.

Lani returned his look for a long, silent moment and then, deliberately, she turned her head and moved across the room in the opposite direction. "Connie," she said, holding out her hand to Dave Yamazaki's plain little wife as if she were a long-lost friend. "How are you?"

Now what the hell was that all about? Wes thought, watching her. What had he done between the time he'd left her at the Sail Away office and now to cause her to give him that freezing, snow-queen look? Surely trying to give her a hand with her problem at Sail Away wouldn't put him in her black books, even if she knew about it. Would it? He shifted uneasily and buried his nose in his drink, think that it very likely would. Ms Lani MacPherson, hell-bent on independence, tended to get on her high horse about the strangest things.

"Would you like another cocktail?" Sumiko asked, ever vigilant to the needs of her guests. "Or an hors d'oeuvre, perhaps? The shrimp toasts are very good," she said, indicating the triangles of deep-fried seafood.

"No thanks," Wes said, his eyes following Lani as she moved from Connie Yamazaki to one of the other wives.

She was very deliberately ignoring him—and making damn sure he knew it. "Neither."

"Is everything quite all right?" Sumiko asked, a small, secret smile in her eyes as she watched him watch her granddaughter. "Has Lani, perhaps, been impolite again?"

"What?" He dragged his eyes from Lani's smooth, bare shoulder, which was all he could see of her at the moment, to look down at the tiny kimono-clad woman beside him. "I'm sorry, what did you say, Mrs. Walsh-san?"

"Has my granddaughter been lacking in hospitality?"

"No, not at all," Wes said, and grinned suddenly, wondering what Sumiko would say if she knew just how hospitable her granddaughter had been. "She's been the soul of amicability," he lied smoothly.

Sumiko nodded agreeably but he knew, somehow, that she didn't believe a word of it. Obviously she knew her granddaughter, too, perhaps better than he did. "Then I will leave you," Sumiko said softly. "I must see to my other guests."

She circulated among the guests, a word here, a smiling nod there, until she was standing, seemingly without meaning to, beside her granddaughter. "You are being impolite to our dear Wesley," she said to Lani.

Lani glared over her grandmother's head at the man in question. "Not as impolite as I'm going to be," she said meaningfully.

Sumiko looked a bit taken aback. "What is wrong, Granddaughter?"

Lani hesitated, not wanting to upset her grandmother. But she's upset me, Lani thought, and, hurting, she wanted to hurt back. She bit her tongue instead.

"Granddaughter?"

"Nothing's the matter, Gran," she said stiffly. "At least, nothing that you don't already know all about." She half turned, unable to talk about it without exploding into a million screaming pieces. "I think Dave is trying to get our attention," she said then, smiling at Dave as he approached them.

What Dave wanted was to invite everyone out to dinner after Sumiko's cocktail party. "I know you do not usually dine out, Mrs. Walsh-san," he said formally. "But, perhaps, in honor of this night?"

"I thank you for the invitation, but I must decline." Sumiko bowed slightly to soften the blow. "My granddaughter, I am sure, will be happy to attend in my place."

"No, I'm sorry, Dave," Lani said, stubbornly ignoring the astonished look on her grandmother's face. "I'm afraid I can't. I've been fighting a rotten headache all day," she improvised, putting a hand to her temple, "and I think it's finally caught up with me. I'm going to make an early night of it," she said. "In fact, I think I'll say goodnight now, before it gets any worse."

"But Granddaughter—" Sumiko began.

"Maybe my grandmother will reconsider, after all," Lani said, adroitly cutting her off without seeming to. "If you'll excuse me?" she said, hurrying through the archway and down the hall to her room before anyone could say another word, biting her lip against the sudden tears that threatened.

She stayed in her room—hiding, she chided herself—until she heard the guests leave. She had no way of knowing if her grandmother had gone with them, of course, but if she hadn't then she'd undoubtedly gone to bed. Late evenings and too many guests tended to tire her these days, which was one of the reasons she didn't dine out.

When the house was still and quiet, Lani opened the glass doors that led to the garden and stepped outside into the soft, dark night. Moving silently, her feet bare, she wandered across the velvety lawn to the *koi* pond. A pale half-moon flickered on its surface, dancing on the little ripples made by the golden fish. Lani sank down on the decorative rock border beside it, her violet *pareau* separating over her knees to brush against the grass. Absently she reached out, drawing aimless circles on the surface of the water.

It was funny, she thought. Funny and frightening and sad how Sail Away suddenly seemed to mean so little to her at the moment. As short a time ago as this morning it had been her number one priority in life to ferret out the mystery behind her company's problems and set them right. Well, now she'd found them out. And where had it gotten her?

Right where she wanted to be, she told herself firmly, but it sounded hollow, even to her own ears. She had lost her absolute faith in her grandmother. She'd been betrayed by two employees. And she'd offered her heart and her trust to a man who deserved neither.

The trust she could take back, but her heart was another matter because, even now, she found herself wishing for what might have been. And there *had* been something there, something real that, given a chance, might have grown into something lasting. But, whatever chance there might have been for them, it was gone now. She would never love a man she couldn't trust. Or, at least, she'd never admit to loving him. She was glad, so glad, that she hadn't admitted it already.

She trailed her fingers through the still, moon-kissed water, feeling drained and utterly apathetic, the brief flush of triumph she had felt in facing down Al completely gone now. Despondency had taken its place.

"I wish," she whispered, evoking the childhood ritual of wishing on the *koi*. "I wish Pop had never left me Sail Away in the first place," she said, totally dispirited. "I wish Gran wasn't such a steel-spined old dowager. I wish Wes—" she stopped, hearing a rustling behind her.

"You wish Wes what?" asked Wes from behind her.

Lani stiffened her spine. "I wish Wes would just get the hell away from me."

Wes sighed. "Aren't you overreacting again?" he said, staring down at the moonlight dancing on her glossy hair. "All I did was drive out to Haliewa and—"

"So you admit it," she said dully. "I didn't think you would."

"Lord, why not?" He crouched down in front of her. Lani turned her head away. "Come on, Moonmaid," he coaxed, reaching out to turn her face to his. "It isn't as if I actually interfered with—"

"Not interfered!" Lani pushed his hand away, trying desperately not to cry. "You call what you did not interfering?"

"Well, maybe a little," he admitted, trying to placate her. She was even angrier than he'd first thought. "But I—" He broke off as a single tear, as large and clear as a diamond, rolled down Lani's averted cheek. "Lani, what is it?"

She brushed at it with the back of her hand, furious with herself. "Nothing."

He tried to draw her into his arms. "Sweetheart, whatever it is that you think I've done, I'm sor—"

She shoved him, knocking him on his backside, and stood up. "Don't call me sweetheart!" she hissed at him. "You . . . you pirate!"

Wes caught himself on his palms. "Pirate?" he said, staring up at her. "What the hell does that mean?"

"You figure it out." She stalked past him.

He caught her bare ankle in his hand. "Hold it a minute, there," he said, squeezing harder when she tried to yank her ankle away. "Just hold it a minute."

She felt his other hand on her thigh, and then her ankle was released, and her waist was grasped, and he was on his feet, standing in front of her, holding her there with his hand around her wrist.

"Just what the hell is this all about?"

Lani tugged at her wrist and glared at him.

"Is this because I finally got through your defenses and—"

"Took advantage of me, you mean!"

"Took *advantage* of you?" He looked mildly outraged. "Of all the ridiculous—" He shook his head. "I can't believe you have the gall to stand here in front of me and say that."

"It's true, dammit!" she hissed.

"It is not true." He shook her captured wrist slightly. "It's ridiculous and you know it. I no more took advantage of you than you did of me." He flung up his free hand in exasperation. "You came to me that first night," he reminded her.

"Let me go," Lani demanded in tones that would have frozen a lesser man.

"I will not," he said, not the least bit intimidated. Puzzled, yes, and a little angry himself now, but not intimidated. "Not until you tell me what your problem is. And I warn you—" his hands shifted to her upper arms and he shook her slightly "—don't give me that crap about taking advantage of you again. We made love to each other. *Love*, do you hear me, woman?"

Lani clamped her teeth shut and refused to answer, fighting the scalding tears that threatened to overflow.

Wes felt all his anger melt in an instant. She looked so defenseless and hurt. But what had he done to hurt her? "Oh, Lord, sweetheart, don't cry."

"Don't call me sweetheart!" she hissed. "I'm not your sweetheart!"

"Yes, you are," he said, trying to comfort her, although he had no idea of what he was comforting her for. He only knew that he had to take that look off her face. He touched her cheek lightly with his fingertip, trailing it up to her temple to gently tuck her hair behind her ear. "You're my one and only sweetheart," he said tenderly. "Don't you know that?"

Lani squeezed her eyes shut. "Oh, Wes, please. Don't pretend anymore. I know all about it."

"All about what?"

Her eyes opened. "All about the scheme you and Gran cooked up with Al," she said dully. "I saw you with—"

"Scheme?" His hand clamped over her upper arm again. "What scheme? Didn't we agree that there wasn't any damned scheme?"

"Al Duffy this afternoon," she continued, ignoring his interruption. "I found out what he was doing and I went to Haliewa to confront him with it. And I saw you."

"Lani, you've misunder—"

"No, please, let me finish. Kim told me everything and—"

"Kim?" Wes was more bewildered than ever. "Who's Kim?"

"My office helper," Lani reminded him. "She told me everything. About how Al forced her to alter the books, and the invoices she threw away, and the deliberately fouled-up bookings." Her shoulders lifted in a pathetic little gesture.

"Everything. Al even showed me that pitiful, trumped up partnership agreement he has."

"And you think I'm involved in that?"

"I *know* you're involved in it, Wes," she said despondently, refusing to meet his eyes. "It's just that I thought, after what happened between us—"

"After we made love, you mean?"

Lani glared at him. "After we had *sex*," she said the word deliberately. "I thought you'd refuse to get involved in any scheme to get Sail Away away from me. But I was wrong, wasn't I?"

"Yes, you were wrong."

Lani looked up at that, surprised by the intense, strangled sound of his voice. His lips were pressed tight, suppressing some emotion that he didn't care, or didn't dare, to let go of. His blue eyes were glittering in the moonlight. His hands on her arms were almost bruising in their intensity. They stared at each other for a long, silent, stress-filled moment and then, suddenly, Wes burst out laughing. It was either that, he thought, or throttle her!

"Dammit, Lani, you're the most stubborn, wrongheaded female. Just what kind of man do you—"

"You're laughing!" she exploded, suddenly furious. Not sad anymore. Not dejected. Not despondent. But gloriously, splendidly furious. And it felt good. It felt marvelous, in fact. Much better than dragging around like some spineless, whiny wimp. Had she actually even thought of giving up Sail Away? Not a chance!

"How can you be so callous?" She twisted in his grasp. "You force me to stand here and bare my soul, and then you have the nerve to laugh!" she spat. Going rigid, she yanked herself out of his hands. "Well, you can stand there and laugh yourself sick for all I care," she said with icy dignity, her tears drying as if they had never been. "I'm going in the house." She turned on her bare heel, intending to do just that.

Wes's hands shot out, grabbing and turning her in mid-motion. She stumbled, flinging out her hands to break her fall, and found herself wrapped securely in his arms. She opened her mouth to curse him but his mouth covered hers, his tongue slipping past her open lips. She tried to hit him, her small fists clenched, intending to do serious damage if she could. He shifted quickly, barely lifting his mouth from hers as his big hands grasped her wrists, one in each hand. He anchored them at the small of her back and arched her into his body.

"Let me g—"

And then his mouth covered hers again. Securely, warmly, wetly, with furious, angry passion. Lani struggled for a moment longer, furious and unbelievably aroused, but the more she strained against his assault, the harder her breasts were pushed against the unyielding wall of his chest. She surrendered suddenly, making a small moaning sound as she went limp in his arms. His kiss changed just as suddenly, less fierce but no less passionate. He loosened his grip on her hands, bit by bit, and then altogether when he realized that she only wanted to use them to embrace him. Her hands lifted to his head, tangling in his hair to pull him closer. His flattened on her back and slid down over the silk of her *pareau*, lifting her into his aroused, straining body.

"Lani," he murmured, breathing raggedly into the soft, scented skin of her neck. "Lani." She felt his mouth move on her throat and shoulders, hot and moist and wanting. "Whatever it is you think I did with Al Duffy, you're wrong," he said between kisses. "I didn't cook up any scheme with him, or conspire with him. I promise you I didn't."

Lani's neck arched, seemingly against her will. "But I saw you," she breathed, wanting desperately to believe him but not quite able to. "I saw you," she whispered, and closed her eyes as he claimed her mouth again.

The kiss was long and sweet and thorough, and when he lifted his mouth, he sighed and pressed his forehead against hers. "You may have seen me with Duffy but it wasn't what you thought. I wasn't conspiring with him. I was trying to find out what he was up to."

Lani's eyes opened wide at that and a fierce joy welled up in her heart, struggling to break through the doubt and distrust. She drew back a little so she could see his expression. "You were?"

"I was," he affirmed. "I mean, what the hell? Everybody seemed to think I was here as Sumiko's hand-picked henchman, anyway, no matter what I said to the contrary. So I thought I might as well take advantage of it. I went over to Haliewa this afternoon to see what I could find out about Al's operation."

"Why?"

"Well, why do you think?" he asked, exasperated. "You were having problems with Sail Away. It didn't seem to be Rich. At least, you didn't seem to think it was. I knew it wasn't your grandmother. Al was the next logical choice. I remembered what you'd said about your father once considering him as a partner and then not going through with it. It sounded as if there might be some bad feelings there. It was worth looking into, anyway."

"Not my grandmother?" she whispered, her joy just about complete. *Not her grandmother!*

It was Wes's turn to draw back a little. "You suspected your grandmother, too?" he chided, and then shook his head. "Shame on you, Lani MacPherson."

"Well, I didn't know what else to think," she defended herself. "Gran's made no secret of the fact that she doesn't want me to run Sail Away. That she wanted me to get married. Then you showed up instead of your Uncle Gerard. And Gran kept pushing us together. And the books were all screwed up and, well, I—" She shrugged.

"Put two and two together and came up with five."

"Something like that, I guess." She lowered her eyes to the knot in his red silk tie. "I feel awful," she said in a small, guilty voice.

Wes grinned his pirate's grin. "Oh, I don't know." He ran his finger down over the curve of her buttocks. "You feel pretty good to me."

Lani gave a watery little giggle and looked up at him from under inky, tear-damp lashes. "This is no time for that," she chided.

"Any time is time."

"No, it isn't." Lani stepped back, sinking to the edge of the *koi* pond again, and she pulled Wes down beside her. "Tell me what you found out about Al," she demanded.

"Not much more than you did." He put his arm around her. "He seems to think that your father owed him something."

"Do you think he did?" Lani said hesitantly. Might her father have actually reneged on a promise?

"I think it's conceivable that your father might have discussed a partnership agreement at some point. Because he needed capital, would be my guess. That's the usual reason. But discussing a partnership isn't the same—"

"Gran bought *Destiner* from him," Lani interrupted.

"What?"

She turned to him excitedly. "Gran holds the title to *Destiner*. About eight, maybe nine years ago Pop wanted to expand the business. Gran wanted to give him the money outright, I think. But Pop insisted that she take *Destiner*."

"That explains it, then." Wes nodded musingly. "Your father got the money he needed without taking on a partner."

"Yes, but he did discuss. Does that mean Al has a case? Could he sue me for part of Sail Away?"

Wes squeezed her shoulders. "He can try, but it won't do him any good. I think he knows that, too. In fact, I think he knew it all along. And that's why he was trying to undermine your business."

"But that doesn't make any sense, Wes. Why would he want to ruin the business if he wanted it?"

"I don't think he intended to ruin it. I think what he wanted to do was discredit you with your vendors and customers and hope that things got to the point where you'd be willing to make some kind of deal. You said yourself that he was from the old school and didn't think much of women. Maybe he thought you'd get so discouraged that you'd sell him the fishing fleet at a good price. Hell, maybe he thought you'd give it to him just to get it off your hands." Wes shrugged. "Who knows?"

Lani laughed softly, sadly. "Poor Al. If he'd just asked, I'd have probably done just that. Made him a good deal, I mean. I've never had a lot of interest in the fishing fleet. It makes money but—" She sighed and leaned her head against Wes's shoulder. "I feel sorry for him in a way."

"How's that?"

"If he'd just waited awhile, he might have gotten exactly what he wanted without all the chicanery."

Wes was quiet for a moment, considering that. "If I just wait awhile, will I get what I want?"

Lani tilted her head to look at him. "And what do you want?"

"You."

Lani sat up straight. "Me?" she said carefully, peering at him in the moonlight. "In what way, exactly?"

"In every way there is."

"What—" she began and then stopped. *In every way there is.* That could mean everything or nothing at all. But she had the feeling that he wasn't going to elaborate until she made a few things clear first. He was asking her to trust him. Something, she realized, that she hadn't done even before she'd seen him with Al.

"A while ago, when I said that we just had sex," she began, staring at her hands, "I was lying. When I said it was only passion, I was lying then, too. To myself, mostly. We made love. Every time, it was love." She looked up at him with her whole heart in her eyes. "I love you, Wesley Adams," she said softly.

"I love you, Leilani MacPherson," he said just as softly. And then he folded her in his arms, lifting her so that she was sitting in his lap. The kiss they shared was deep and sweet and full of promise.

"When will you marry me?" he asked when they stopped for breath.

"What about your cruise to Tahiti or Africa or wherever?"

"We'll still go if you want to. On our honeymoon, maybe. Or we'll stay here and run Sail Away together. Or maybe you'll run Sail Away, and I'll open the Hawaiian branch of Adams & Adams. Who knows? We can figure that out as we go along."

"I thought you wanted to get away from it all?"

"What I wanted was a change of scene, a lot of sailing and a chance to try something different for a while." He grinned suddenly. "Marrying you will certainly be different."

"Wes!" Lani tried to sound insulted but her smile ruined it.

"So," he said, serious again. "Will you marry me, Leilani?"

Lani smiled into his eyes. "You'll have to ask my grandmother about that."

"What?"

"She's Japanese, you know—very old-fashioned," Lani said primly. "I have to get her permission and she—" Lani squealed, clutching Wes's neck as he came to his feet with her in his arms.

He kissed her, hard and fast, barely giving her enough time to kiss him back. His pirate's grin flashed. His eyes glowed with triumph and love and laughter. "Let's go ask her," he said. And then he shifted his burden, tossing Lani over his shoulder like a battle prize, and strode across the garden to the house.

SUMIKO WALSH, standing in the shadows of the lanai, turned quickly toward the house, hiding a pleased smile. She hurried toward her late husband's den and the book that she would pretend to have been reading when they came to tell her their joyous news. It wouldn't do to have the children know that she had been watching them. But it made her heart so happy, now that her granddaughter was acting as a proper woman should. She couldn't wait until they had gone to bed so that she could call Gerard and tell him the good news.

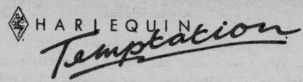

HARLEQUIN Temptation

COMING NEXT MONTH

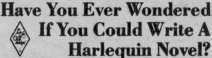

Have You Ever Wondered If You Could Write A Harlequin Novel?

Here's great news—Harlequin is offering a series of cassette tapes to help you do just that. Written by Harlequin editors, these tapes give practical advice on how to make your characters—and your story—come alive. There's a tape for each contemporary romance series Harlequin publishes.

Mail order only

All sales final

ANNOUNCING . . .

The Lost Moon Flower
by Bethany Campbell

Look for it this August
wherever Harlequins are sold